OPERATION TENLEY

THE FAIR CITY FILES

BOOK ONE

JENNIFER GOOCH HUMMER

Month9Books

THE FAIR CITY FILES: OPERATION TENLEY by Jennifer Gooch Hummer
All rights reserved. Published in the United States of America by Month9Books, LLC.
No part of this book may be used or reproduced in any manner whatsoever without written permission of the publisher, except in the case of brief quotations embodied in critical articles and reviews.

ISBN: 978-1-942664-99-4

Published by Month9Books, Raleigh, NC 27609
Cover design by Ampersand Book Covers at www. ampersandbookcovers.com

Month9Books

PRAISE FOR OPERATION TENLEY

"If Holly Short from Artemis Fowl was trying to rehabilitate Veruca Salt from Willie Wonka while battling Mother Nature and her Heat/Snow Miser sons, you'd have the Fair City Files. Quirky characters and rollicking fun."—Dianne K. Salerni, author of *The Eighth Day* Series

"If you like stories with fairies, you'll love *Operation Tenley* where futuristic fairies are tasked with guarding earth's teens who have gained elemental powers, risking the ire and wrath of Mother Nature. With a fun, high-stakes battle for control over the planets elements, it's sure to please middle-grade readers."—Alane Adams, award-winning author of *The Red Sun* and *Kalifus Rising*

"A fun, fresh mash-up of magic and technology. This is one modern twist on fairies you won't want to miss!"—Tobie Easton author of *Emerge*

Madison, Daisy, Tatum, and, Craig
Dragons are real.

OPERATION

TENLEY

THE FAIR CITY FILES

BOOK ONE

1

Hadley Beach, California

Tenley Tylwyth needed votes.

Which is why today she stood outside in the busy quad wearing a sash draped over her left shoulder that read *Vote For Me, Tenley T!*

Behind her, a group of boys played Frisbee, while in front of her, students hurried by, ignoring the flyers she held out.

Please **totally** Nominate Tenley Tylwyth to
represent Hadley Middle School on
America's Next Most Inspirational Teen
this Friday Night

When the Frisbee flew straight toward Tenley's head, none of the students noticed.

Except one.

Holden Wonderbolt was a size or two skinnier than the other boys his age, with milk chocolate skin and impressive skateboard skills. He was on the way to the skate ramp when he spotted the Frisbee.

"Watch out!" he yelled.

Tenley turned around just as Holden leaped off his board and launched himself forward. Instead of intercepting the Frisbee, though, Holden sailed toward Tenley while above them, the Frisbee spun off in the opposite direction.

Had others seen it, they would have wondered: *Did that Frisbee just stop in midair, flip itself sideways, and zoom off in a completely different direction?* But no one had seen it. Not even Holden, who was busy preparing to land on Tenley.

This is what Tenley did: step back.

This is what Holden did: (crash) land.

This is what the rest of the students did: stare.

Oh, and a few photos were taken and posted on the Internet within seconds.

2

North West Observation Spot, Fair City

Standard Fair One 3^{rd}i's were sufficient enough to see everything happening on Earth, even from the far edge of Fair City. But Laraby must have missed something. Why would his client ditch his skateboard and dive toward another student like that?

He tapped at his 3^{rd}i and groaned, then flung it back over his head into its holder. "Piece of junk. A 3^{rd}i-All wouldn't have missed anything," he mumbled. Laraby coveted 3^{rd}i-Alls, which were infinitely better, but were only issued to Lieutenant Fair Ones.

Frustrated, he rubbed his bald head and stepped back over jagged rocks and dust, the latter of which was always the archenemy of his pristine white robes. He pulled a controller out of his tool belt and entered some information. A small hologram screen appeared. A few more clicks and the scene he had just watched on Earth projected in front of him.

There was Holden, skateboarding through the quad, when suddenly and without reason, he flung himself off and dived straight into an unsuspecting girl. Nothing in Holden's immediate surroundings gave any indication of potential danger. Wind, humidity, barometric pressure, fire, temperature, tectonic plates—all normal.

Laraby pulled his eyes off the screen and sighed. Today he was not in the mood. He'd been hoping to grab a small bite, and now his client's potential injury would eat into his lunch hour. He'd have to fill out an accident report, for one thing, and Holden Wonderbolt was getting dangerously close to his limit. Another injury could very well result in a red flag for Laraby, which might then lead to a review. And although Laraby did quite enjoy Holden Wonderbolt, he had to admit the boy was a bit of a klutz.

Laraby prepared for departure. The sooner he submitted the report, the better. City Hall was becoming ever more crowded and less efficient.

Just as his propellers started to activate, a loud whirring sound made him take pause. There was nothing wrong with his equipment, as far as he could tell. No damage that he could recall, and he was always on top of the updates. But the whirring noise increased. Perhaps it was another Fair One coming to share his ob-spot. This seemed to be happening more frequently, even though he always picked the farthest, most remote sites to observe his client.

Or perhaps it was asteroid winds picking up. He'd heard talk the last time he was in City Hall that Mother Nature and her Weathers were on the brink of infiltrating the Fair Force's protective layer again. A stronger system had been implemented since her first infiltration, but no one knew if this was enough. Mother Nature and her Weathers were becoming increasingly hostile, which meant the clients on Earth were in even more danger. Time spent filling out injury reports was precious time away from monitoring them.

Dust picked up around him. He'd washed his robes only yesterday. Annoyed, Laraby stepped out of the swirling debris but stopped when an enormous wind tunnel appeared overhead, close enough to be dangerous. With no time to protect his gear, Laraby took cover under his arms, abruptly knocking the 3rdi sideways. He yelped. A Fair One's tools were powerful but not indestructible and once damaged, were never quite the same.

He waited for impact, but nothing happened. He peeked up at Fair Force, three of them, hovering a few meters above. Their badges were visible, and red sirens flashed over their propellers.

"Fair One LARA B3. You are under arrest. Anything you think can and will be used against you. You are hereby ordered to City Hall in three minutes. Failure to do so will result in further penalty."

"Officers," Laraby shouted above the noise. "I think you must be mistaken."

The Fair Force typed into a small tablet. A pocket in Laraby's tool belt buzzed. The arrest warrant was delivered.

City Hall in *three minutes*? He'd never been arrested before.

"Good day," the Fair Force nodded, before propelling upward and zooming away as fast as they had come.

"It's *lunch* time," Laraby grumbled, activating his propellers again. As soon as he felt his feet lift, he tipped his head left and started for City Hall.

3

South West Observation Spot, Fair City

Pennie pushed back her 3rdi to focus on that sound. Just as she thought, it was getting closer: a deep humming that vibrated enough to make the inside of her ears itch.

She felt around her white robes for her tool belt. Her inquiry about smaller-sized robes had gone unanswered. And so today, as she did every other day, she looked like a basket of laundry with red hair.

She found her location device and clicked on it. She was right where she thought she was, on one of the more remote ob-spots where few Fair Ones ever went. In fact, most believed this particular ob-spot was still shut down, the aftermath of a small turf warfare between Administratives and Fair Force. Why the Administratives ever thought they could win was anyone's guess.

Pennie slipped the location device back into her tool belt. When she looked up again, a wind tunnel was getting closer. Heading straight toward her, in fact.

She started to activate her propellers, but the wind tunnel slammed to a halt above her. Three figures with badges and red lights flashing above them unraveled.

"Fair One PENN 1? You are under arrest. Anything you think can and will be used against you. You are hereby ordered to City Hall in three minutes. Failure to do so will result in further penalty."

The Fair Force typed into his small tablet. Pennie's tool belt buzzed. Her arrest warrant was delivered.

She shook her head. She'd never been arrested before. "Officers, I'm in the middle of monitoring my client. It's not really a convenient time. Would it be okay if I came in tomorrow?"

The biggest of the Fair Force dropped closer. "No." He pulled out a set of handcuffs.

Pennie stepped back. "Actually, on second thought, I'm all done here. Thank you, Officers."

"I suggest you get on your way then, Fair One."

The three Fair Force lifted upward and zoomed away.

"I was just doing my *job*," Pennie mumbled, activating her propellers properly this time. As soon as she was off the ground, she tipped her head right and started toward City Hall.

4

Fair City

Pennie rarely had a clean landing and this time was no different. She stumbled and yelped before falling back on her buttocks.

It was her feet. Because along with their smallish four-foot stature, a Fair One also possessed tiny feet—not particularly good for landing. Descendants of the fairies of yesteryear, whose ancestors had wings for transportation, a Fair One no longer possessed these magical limbs. They did, however, maintain the same tiny feet, which presented a challenge. Wings and tiny feet allowed for a delicate landing, but *propellers* and tiny feet did not. Experienced Fair Ones may have perfected the act, but graceful landings required a skill that rookie Fair Ones like Pennie had yet to master.

Fair City was buzzing today. Fair Ones were coming and

going, and collisions were constant. The danger of so many propellers had at one time been enough for the Fairships to ban them in town altogether. But Fair Ones were busy, and getting busier, and walking simply took too long. So eventually propellers were reinstated, and now there was hardly ever a Fair One on tiny foot.

Pennie retracted her propellers and looked at the building ahead.

City Hall was written above the entrance. It was a drab building. Once gleaming like everything else in Fair City, it was now covered in layers of dust and debris.

A sign by the bottom stair read:

NO OPEN PROPELLERS
PAST THIS POINT

Pennie gathered her robes and began climbing the stairs.

A dozen meters away on the other side of the grand staircase, Laraby had little trouble landing. Laraby was an overachiever and the first of his family to become a Fair One. His parents and siblings had no desire to work for the Fairships. They chose instead to live well outside of Fair City on another bit of space junk in the asteroid belt where they quietly manufactured propeller parts—except for one of his brothers, whom he preferred not to think about at the moment. Or any other moment.

Laraby reached down for his tool belt, braced himself while his propellers retracted, and brushed down his long red beard.

Then he, too, gathered his robes and started climbing.

Halfway up the staircase, Pennie noticed a disheveled Fair One sitting alone. His robes were tarnished with soot and grime, and a few bits and parts of an old propeller were cupped in between his palms. A sign by his feet read: *Blade-less. Please help.*

"Extra blades?" he asked hopefully. Pennie slowed. Something about his eyes reminded her of her father, who had gone on a galactic tour with some friends and never returned. Their travel box had hit a meteor. Her mother had never been the same.

Pennie shook her head at the disheveled Fair One. "I'm sorry, sir. I don't have any."

Extra propellers were nearly impossible to come by. The Fair Force kept tight control over all equipment, most *especially* propellers. Unapproved travel outside the asteroid belt was strictly prohibited but somehow becoming more frequent. Perhaps this was why she was getting called in; the ob-spot she'd been on was at the very end of the belt.

"I'll keep my eyes open though," Pennie told him.

"Thank you. And *may His return be swift.*" The Fair One raised his right hand with fingers crossed and pressed it to his heart.

"*May His return be swift,*" Pennie repeated, doing the same with her hand before continuing up the stairs.

Most of the Fair Ones on the staircase were descending, but a few were climbing, their robes gathered into fists and their lungs heaving just like Pennie's. She wasn't used to this level of exertion. A bead of sweat ran down her temple.

At the top, Pennie noticed a bald Fair One with a long red beard stepping up to the landing at the same time she did. They arrived at the entrance at the same time, and noticing her panting, the Fair One held the door for her.

"Thank you," Pennie said.

"Your last remembering is their first vision," he mumbled.

"What?"

Laraby looked up at her, confused. "Did I just say that out loud?"

Pennie smiled politely and stepped inside.

ATTENTION!

DUE TO RECENT ACTIVITY
ALL TOOL BELTS **MUST NOW** BE CHECKED
BEFORE ENTERING THE GREAT HALL
Code 00090.
(ABSOLUTELY NO OPEN PROPELLERS)

Pennie stopped. Hand over her tools? She couldn't hand over her tools. Without them, she'd lose all monitoring capabilities of her client. If there was one thing a rookie learned in training, it was to always keep one's tools close. A Fair One had to be ready at all times.

"Excuse me," Laraby said, stepping around Pennie and up to the Tool Belt Check. Pennie watched him unbuckle his belt and hand it over to the teen Administrator with an eyebrow piercing.

"Thanks," the teen sneered. "LARA B3?" she confirmed, waving his belt over the scanner.

"I am, indeed," Laraby answered.

She handed Laraby the paper ticket that spit out from the scanner. "Listen for your number." She motioned to the door behind him.

Laraby turned around. Pennie was standing in the same place with the same blank look on her face. "We have to give them *all of* our tools?" she asked. "This wasn't anywhere in the Manual."

She looked like she might cry. And crying was something that Laraby just couldn't deal with. He'd grown up with twenty-seven younger siblings, and the last thing he needed right now was to miss his number being called.

He started walking past her.

"Excuse me, do we have to give them *everything*?" Pennie asked him directly this time.

Laraby stopped. "Are you a rookie?"

The Fair One nodded. This rookie was definitely about to cry.

Guilt flooded his senses. He'd been a rookie Fair One not long ago himself.

"It's a new rule. You have to check your entire belt. They won't let you in any farther if you don't. Sets off the alarms."

These words did little to soften Pennie's worried look. Maybe, Laraby thought, she'd been hit in the head by an asteroid particle. That had happened to one of his little sisters, and she'd looked worried ever since. He pointed up to the sign.

"Tool belt. Check. It."

Finally, Pennie shook her head. "Sorry. I feel a little dizzy." She lifted her hand to her forehead. Maybe it was all those stairs.

"I realize," Laraby said, *over-pro-nun-ci-ating* for her just in case she was too dizzy to hear him. "It goes against the natural instinct to give up your tools. You've been trained well. But, like I said, it's a new rule. She's going to scan your belt and give you a ticket. Listen for the number on it—that's how they'll call you up. When you're finished with your business here, you'll hand the ticket back to her and get your belt. Easy."

"What if something happens? I can't fail this assignment."

"Hopefully nothing will. And anyway, you've been summoned here. They can't fail you for that."

Pennie unbuckled her belt and handed it over.

The teen didn't bother making eye contact when she waved Pennie's tool belt over the scanner and handed her the ticket.

Pennie turned to Laraby, who was noticing that the teen still hadn't put his tool belt into a locker. "Thanks," Pennie said. "I don't even know why I'm here."

"Actually, I have no idea why I'm here, either." Laraby narrowed his eyes on the teen Administrator. Finally, she placed their belts into lockers. "Just got summoned a few minutes ago," he continued, glancing at his ticket and pulling open one side of the double doors. "I'm sure it's a mistake, though. I've never broken a rule. After you." He waved Pennie through.

5

Fair City

The Great Hall spread out into a sea of white robes in front of them. Hologram signs floated, bounced, or blinked as far as Pennie and Laraby could see.

Propeller License Renewal Discrepancies?
We can help.
Dial 176.4999.99003 for a free consultation.

Fair One Caught Bending?
You'll need some defense.
Dial 176.4999.99123

"Where do we go?" Pennie's eyes glided over the long lines of Fair Ones snaked around red laser ropes. A plump Fair One with a sticker stuck to his robes bumped into her: **Ask Me How I Lost Weight.**

"Follow me," Laraby said, leading her directly through a blinking hologram sign:

WHEN YOUR ROBES
NEED TO LOOK THEIR VERY BEST
DIAL GALACTIC CLEANERS

"Shortcut," he said, noticing Pennie's surprised look. "There's no rule that says you can't walk through them."

Along the walls as far as Pennie could see, plastic chairs were occupied with bored or bothered-looking Fair Ones, all wearing the same white robes hanging loosely around them now that their tool belts were gone. She had never been around so many Fair Ones at once. During her training, Pennie kept mostly to herself unless she was back at Fair One quarters, where she had a few rookie friends she might meet for dinner or occasionally join for an approved spin around the atmosphere. But space travel made her queasy so she'd usually bow out, claiming she'd had a long day watching over her client and had to be up again early to do the same. The truth was, Pennie spent more time monitoring her client than any of her fellow rookies. She couldn't understand how they could be so relaxed. Danger was everywhere for the clients on Earth.

Pennie followed Laraby past a *General Information* window and over to a long line that ended next to a trash bin.

Laraby took his place at the back of the line.

Pennie lined up behind him. "Is it possible that they could arrest you for doing your job *too* well?"

"No." Laraby shook his head.

The two Fair Ones standing in front of them turned to each other. "It *wasn't* a bad propeller. I distribute *quality* products," the bigger Fair One with a bruised lower lip said.

"Your product is *flawed*." The smaller one poked him.

Laraby turned back to Pennie. "I have heard they've started doing random reviews, though."

"You think we're getting *reviewed*?" Pennie felt dizzy again. "How can I be getting reviewed? I'm still in my rookie assignment. Plus, a review can take a few days. I can't leave my client that long—"

The bigger Fair One in front of them poked the smaller one back. "You're dreamin', old fairy."

"Oh so *that's* what you do, make it everyone else's problem?" The smaller one poked again.

The two were about to come to blows until, "*Taking number 33,000,601,*" was called over the loudspeaker.

"You got lucky," the bigger Fair One mumbled, starting toward the service window.

"*You* got lucky," the smaller one said, hustling to keep up with him.

A Fair One with a slushie cart passed through the space the two fighting Fair Ones had vacated.

"I think I'll get a snack while we're waiting," Laraby said, turning to follow him. Pennie noticed Laraby's large-ish belly. If a Fair One could no longer fit into his tool belt, he was forced to trade in his sleek propellers for a heftier version that moved half as fast. Pennie's belt was too big for her, even on the very last hole.

A siren blared. Pennie covered her ears. The two furious Fair Ones were punching each other. Surrounding Fair Ones scrambled out of their way as three Fair Force with navy-blue tool belts and vests propelled downward from their posts in the ceiling, red lights swirling above their heads.

In an instant, the Fair Ones were handcuffed and lifted up through a door in the ceiling.

Laraby seemed unfazed when he returned with two blue slushies. "I got you one, just in case," he smiled through blue teeth.

"Thanks," Pennie said. "I'm not thirsty, though."

"Try it. City Hall has the best slushies in all of Fair City." Laraby took a sip from his spoon straw. "Plus, you get a free stroon."

Pennie tried a small stroonful. It was delicious, but her stomach was too nervous for more. She'd been gone from Tenley Tylwyth for too long. "Is it usually this busy in here?"

Laraby nodded wide-eyed as he slurped another stroonful. Slushies always managed to improve his mood. "You wouldn't believe how many Fair Ones aren't following the Manual," he raised his eyebrows. "Like the rules weren't put in place for a reason, right?"

Pennie nodded. But who was she kidding? Like most Fair Ones, she'd studied the *Official Fair One Manual* to pass the written exams, but hadn't cracked it open since. In fact, she didn't even know where hers was.

Laraby took his last stroonful and threw the cup into the trash can. *Keep Our Higher Courts Clean* was written on yellow crime-scene tape all around the bin, which featured a picture of two perfectly coiffed redhaired Fair Ones and their shiny new propellers looking proudly down on Earth. *Protecting Clients is Job #1* was written inside a floating bubble above them.

The sunny pictures didn't fool anyone, though. It was no secret that Mother Nature had been orchestrating natural disasters with record frequency. The Fairships claimed to have things under control but the Fair Ones knew better. Ever since the Superintendent of Planet Earth had failed to return from what was supposed to be a quick vacation, humans had been exposed to Mother Nature's growing wrath. She refused to claim responsibility for the earthquakes, floods, and forest fires that had begun taking human lives in frightening quantities, but that was impossible to believe. She wanted revenge. Humans had been destroying her Earth for too long and now with the Super away, she had her chance. As long as she was careful not to attract the attention of Superintendents from any of the other planets, she could quietly reduce the human population. Or even, some believed, eradicate it altogether.

Pennie glanced up. *May His Return Be Swift* was written above a gigantic hologram clock that never stopped counting the days, hours, minutes, and seconds that the Superintendent had been gone: **32506 days, 2 hours, 6 minutes, and 31 seconds.**

Eighty-nine years.

And counting.

At first, when the Super failed to return from vacation on time, it was assumed that inclement galaxy weather was to blame. There was no reason to worry; the Super had stored enough Universal Source Energy (USE) for just this kind of emergency. The fairies could go on doing what they did; granting miracles, fulfilling wishes, doling out lucky breaks, and so on. Until the distressing number of natural disasters began. Then, rather than wishes and miracles, the fairies needed to protect humans from harm. And for that, they relied on large amounts of USE, which was rapidly diminishing. Only the Superintendents of the many different planets were given access to the highly guarded USE. So after weeks and then months of no word from the Earth's Super, during which time the fairies' wings began to break off, panic set in.

Search parties made up of the strongest fairies were sent and returned without success. Finally, they could wait no longer. The Superintendent's right-hand fairies—those who had been left in charge, known as The Original Eights—were forced to come up with a plan. A different energy source had to be used to keep humans safe. And so, after days of difficult and complicated meetings, a plan formed.

Technology.

It would save the world after all.

While Mother Nature continued her onslaught of disasters, the fairies began to harness galactic electrical energy, mostly comprised of cosmic rays and other high-speed particles that travel faster than eighty-seven times the speed of light. Combined with other kinetic and magnetic energies, they were able to create tools so advanced they could even be effective from their asteroid belt in outer space. With these tools, a Fair One—as the fairies would now be called—could monitor and protect their clients—as humans would now be called—almost as well as they could with USE. The Protection Plan wasn't perfect. Tools, after all, can rust and break. But it was the best The Original Eights and their Fair Force could do until the Super finally returned.

If he returned.

Because although everyone still hoped for his swift return, after so much time away, it was becoming more difficult to believe. Some argued he had simply abandoned them. Others were more suspicious, citing jealous Supers from other less dynamic planets who may have wanted to watch Earth fall back into a barren state, leaving their own planets to shine the brightest.

The thought of all that history made Pennie restless. Her client could be in trouble right now. She sighed at the perfect image of the smiling Fair Ones and threw her slushie into the bin.

"Whoa, whoa," Laraby protested, reaching in for her stroon. "Never know when you might be needing one of those." He slipped the stroon into his pocket and stepped back in line. Another number was called over the loudspeaker.

"That's me." Laraby held up his ticket and flashed a quick smile. "Good luck, Fair One."

"You too, and thanks." Pennie watched Laraby disappear into the crowd. Another number was called. This time, it was hers. *Please proceed to Window B.*

"Excuse me," Pennie said, navigating through Fair Ones on her way to the window.

When she reached Window B, she found it occupied by a bald Fair One. With a long red beard.

"Hello again."

He turned around. Then frowned. "You must have the wrong window. And there seems to be no one at this one anyway." He tucked his head in through the empty space to make sure.

"But it said 'B.'" Pennie double-checked her ticket.

"That's not possible."

Pennie pursed her lips.

An Administrator appeared behind the window.

"Finally," Laraby groaned.

Dark circles underlined the Administrator's eyes and a dustnut crumb stuck to his chin. He looked exhausted and angry, like every other Administrator. No longer eligible for Fair One status or equipment manufacturing, usually due to one crime or another, and never even considered for Fair Force, these descendants of fairies had no choice but to remain stationed as Administrators. Unless of course they wanted to join the sipLips, a filthy, ragtag group of scavengers that refused to be anything else.

"Tickets," the Administrator mumbled.

Laraby handed his over directly. Pennie placed hers on the counter. "There's been some mistake," Laraby said. "We seem to have the same citation numbers."

"Well, let's take a little look-see."

Pennie thought she saw a quick roll of Laraby's eyes.

Administrators were not always the sharpest tool in the shed.

"Identities?"

"PENN 1."

"LARA B3."

The Administrator clucked his tongue and typed into his hologram keyboard. A floating report appeared in front of him, which neither Pennie nor Laraby could see.

"No mistake. Same illegal use of Renegade Weathers."

"I beg your pardon?" Laraby said. "I did no such thing. I've never seen this Fair One before. And I've never enlisted the help of a Renegade Weather."

The Administrator replied with a blank face.

Laraby turned to Pennie.

"Don't look at me, I didn't use one either," she said.

Laraby crossed his arms and stared at her.

She lifted her shoulders and dropped them again, defiantly.

Satisfied, Laraby turned back to the Administrator. "So. There you have it. Clean slate?"

The Administrator entered something into the hologram screen. "Nope. According to Fair Force, you've both received a red flag and an official warning. One more infraction, you lose a tool. Good day."

"Listen, *Sir*," Laraby clenched his jaw. "I guess you didn't *hear* what we just *said*. Neither one of us used a Renegade Weather."

The Administrator grinned. "What's that now? You want *two* red flags? Done." He tapped on his keyboard.

Laraby grabbed the Administrator's arm through the window. "You can't *do* that. I have a *perfect* record."

Pennie snuck a look up at the Fair Force in their posts. "Let him go," she warned.

Laraby loosened his hold. The Administrator extracted himself from his grip.

"Please," Laraby said evenly. "Take those warnings off my record. Or I'll report *you*."

The Administrator interwove his fingers together. "I'm sorry. But I do not have the authority—"

Laraby reached for his arm again. "You just *added* one without authority. Now take them both *off*."

Above, one of the Fair Force was watching them.

"Come on." Pennie tapped Laraby's shoulder. "We'll come back later."

Laraby shrugged Pennie off. The Administrator glared at him. "If you don't walk away right now, Fair One, I will call Fair Force."

"LARA B3. Don't. It's not worth it," Pennie pointed upwards. "They're watching."

Laraby took in a deep breath—just before snapping up the Administrator's keyboard and yanking it out through the window

The security alarm blared. Two Fair Force dropped from the ceiling with stun guns drawn.

"Take them to Room Thirty-three," the Administrator ordered.

"But I didn't—" Pennie started to argue.

"*Both* of them."

The Fair Force nodded, and in an instant Pennie and Laraby were lifted through the ceiling.

24

6

Fair City

Room 33 was empty but for two plastic chairs in the middle and a long white countertop with two elaborately decorated thrones behind it.

A recorded voice sounded: *"Please take a seat. Someone will be with you shortly."*

Laraby started for the plastic chairs. "It's unacceptable that Administration is allowed any form of punitive authority over us. I'm sure this will be cleared up quickly, PENN 1."

"It's Pennie. And I'm guessing they *can* punish us, considering you tried to rip that Administrator's arm off. It was just a red flag, LARA—"

"*Laraby*. And I beg your pardon, but I had a *perfect record. Have*." He sat. "Which is beside the point. Administration is made up of bookkeepers, pencil pushers, form-fillers. That's the entirety of their job description. *Not* doling out punishments. If they'd wanted to become Fair Force, or do *our* jobs, they should have thought about that long before doing whatever it is they did to get them where they are now."

Pennie sat next to him. "Why isn't anyone here?"

A light snapped on above the white counter and an elderly Fairship with a red beard three times the length of Laraby's walked directly out of the wall.

He didn't look particularly friendly—until you compared him to the *next* elderly Fairship who stepped through the wall. She was slightly taller with red hair pulled into a bun and a severe face that, like it or not, was still quite beautiful. Their robes were crisp and white. As the highest commanders of the Fair Force, Fairships did not wear tool belts and their unwrinkled robes proved it.

"These aren't just Fairships. They're *Lord* and *Lady* Fairships; *Original Eights*," Laraby said quietly.

"How do you know?" Pennie watched the two sit on their thrones.

"Their sleeves."

It was true. Both had bell sleeves adorned with red cuffs. The only Original Eights Pennie had ever seen before were in her Manual. She had seen one or two Fairships, recognizable by their orange cuffs, propelling around Fair City on rare occasion. But Original Eights stayed out of the public eye.

A third figure stepped out of a solid door to the left side of the wall. He was younger and less impressive-looking, and his bell sleeves were lined with yellow cuffs.

"That's a Higher-Up," Laraby whispered.

"One of them came to talk to my rookie class," Pennie remembered. He'd explained to the class that as an assistant to the Fairships, a Higher-Up could eventually become a Fairship, but most preferred to remain where they were, counting numbers and creating spreadsheets.

"Good day, Lord and Lady Fairship," the Higher-Up bowed from the end of the counter where he stood.

"And to you," Lord Fairship responded brightly.

Lady Fairship offered only a small pull of her lips.

"And good day to you, Fair Ones." Lord Fairship acknowledged them. "Now let's begin. You two have been brought to us on suspicion of Bending. Using Renegade Weathers. Is this correct?"

Laraby shook his head. "I'm afraid there's been a mistake, your Fairship."

"Excellent. Let's hope there is." He nodded. "We'll take a look."

The Higher-Up tapped on his tablet and a large hologram screen appeared on the right side of the room. "Please remain still, Fair One," he ordered.

A red laser dot appeared on Laraby's forehead. It travelled down and then left across his red eyebrow, finally settling on the temporal lobe two inches above his left cheekbone. Pennie squirmed in her seat but Laraby remained stiff. He shifted his eyes toward the screen without moving his head. The lights went out.

There's Holden, outside in the quad, minding his own business, practicing a few moves on his skateboard, when something catches his eye: a Frisbee heading straight for a girl passing out flyers. He launches off his board to intercept the Frisbee. He misses and nearly lands on the girl, who steps back just in time.

The screen froze and the dot disappeared from Laraby's temporal lobe. The lights snapped on.

Pennie frowned. How was this scene in Laraby's memory? How did he know Tenley Tylwyth?

"We cannot confirm that Fair One LARA B3 enlisted Renegade Weathers here," the Higher-Up announced after tapping his tablet a few more times.

"Because I didn't!" Laraby threw his hands up. "Like I already told that Administrator down there, I've never enlisted Renegade Weathers for the protection of my client, or for any other reason. Ever. I protect my client with my tools, as archaic as some of them are. I didn't even use *those* in this circumstance. My client was not in any danger."

The Higher-Up agreed. "From this report, your Fairships, not a single one of his tools was used to manipulate the flying device."

"Frisbee," Laraby corrected him.

"Frisbee." The Higher-Up nodded, making the change in his tablet.

Lord Fairship looked pleased. "This is good news. We should remind you anyway that using Renegade Weathers is a serious bending. Although Renegade Weathers may come across as harmless, they are still a part of Mother Nature's army, however estranged. They can turn on us and your client at any moment.

Our Fair Force does the best job they can of dissolving these Weathers before Mother Nature can recapture them, but it's quite difficult and requires a substantial amount of USE."

"I understand, your Fairship." Laraby stood. "So may I go?"

"There is still the matter of threatening an Administrator," Lady Fairship said.

"It was his fault!" Laraby argued.

"Be careful, Fair One LARA B3. If security is called, this will count as your third red flag," Lady Fairship warned.

Laraby dipped his head. "Your Fairships, if I may, Rule 2938 in the Manual states that any punitive action given by an Administrator requires a review before being implemented."

The Higher-Up nodded regretfully. "He is correct, Lady Fairship. Would you like me to add this to your calendar? I can see you have a little time after dinner."

"No," Lady Fairship said. "I'm afraid I have a previous engagement."

"Very well, which is ..." The Higher-Up started to click on Lady Fairship's calendar.

"Which is something that I'd rather not discuss here."

"I'm afraid I won't have time for another review today either," Lord Fairship said. "Asteroid Golf."

"Your Fairships," Laraby said quickly. "Becoming a Lieutenant Fair One has been my goal for as long as I can remember. These red flags will prevent me from reaching it. I am sorry for the incident with the Administrator. But if you will please allow me to keep my perfect record, I will gladly volunteer to tutor rookies with their Manual exams."

Lord Fairship turned to the Higher-Up. "I'll allow it," he nodded. At Lady Fairship's look, he said quietly, "We are short of Lieutenants as it is. Any aspirations for a rise in ranks should be welcomed."

Lady Fairship tightened her mouth but stayed silent.

"Thank you, your Fairships."

"We will need you to stay while we move onto the next Fair One," Lord Fairship said. "Let's hope we find good news here too."

"Let's hope," Laraby mumbled, sitting again.

A red laser dot appeared on Pennie's forehead. She tipped her head back to see it.

"Please refrain from facial movements and sit flush against your chair, Fair One PENN 1," the Higher-Up ordered.

Pennie scooted back and froze. The dot travelled the same way it had on Laraby's head, ending on her temporal lobe, just below her left ear.

The screen blinked on again. Pennie turned her head to look at it. The screen went fuzzy.

"We need you to *please* keep still," the Higher-Up repeated.

"Unless you'd prefer a skull cage?" Lady Fairship offered.

Pennie shook her head but stopped when she realized she shouldn't have.

The screen blipped on again.

Tenley Tylwyth stands in the middle of the quad passing out flyers. "Vote for me, Tenley T!" She smiles at her fellow students, none of whom pay any attention to her. Tenley remains

30

undeterred. "That's right, people. I'm running for America's Next Most Inspirational Teen. And I need your vote, Hadley Beach!"

The school bell rings.

Tenley looks over her shoulder, affording her a peripheral view of the Frisbee heading straight for her. She blows out a quick breath and watches as the Frisbee heads off in the other direction ... until something even bigger comes flying toward her. A boy. She steps back just before he lands on her. The boy hits the cement with a hard thud.

The screen froze.

Pennie looked pale.

"Now your Lordships," the Higher-Up said without turning the lights on. "If we slow this same scene and magnify the Frisbee, this is what we get."

The Frisbee, just before reaching Tenley's head, comes to a complete stop, hovers, flips over, and zooms out of frame in the opposite direction.

The lights returned.

"It was me!" Pennie blurted out. "I used my iWind to interrupt the Frisbee's trajectory. It was heading straight for my client's left cheek. I should have let the Frisbee stay on its course. Seeing it again, like that, up there, I can tell that it was not, well probably not, an attack by Mother Nature. It looks more like, you know, normal daily activity, which I know we are not meant to interfere with. I'm a rookie your Fairships, I guess I

31

overreacted. It won't happen again. I'll take the penalty."

Laraby frowned over at her. She was talking a mile a minute. The Higher-Up frowned at her too and then clicked on his tablet.

"Give us a moment, Fair One," he said.

"What's your problem?" Laraby leaned into her while the Higher-Up and the Fairships conversed in a huddle. "Why are you talking so fast?"

"I'm not. I wasn't." Pennie tapped her feet.

"Unfortunately," the Higher-Up turned back to them. "Despite what you've just told us, we cannot find any evidence of *your* tools being used either, Fair One PENN 1."

Pennie stood. "What? No, I definitely programmed the iWind—"

"Sit," Lady Fairship said. "Perform the deep memory excavation," she instructed the Higher-Up.

"Your Fairship," he argued, "may I remind you that the deep memory laser uses five hundred times the USE that review lasers do. I would suggest that we don't waste supply on smaller matters."

"She's lying," Lady Fairship turned to Lord Fairship. "We cannot have Fair Ones telling lies. This is a perfect example of what I was saying at our last meeting."

"I'll allow it." Lord Fairship nodded to the Higher-Up.

Pennie sat forward. "Please don't waste the USE on me."

"Sit back, Fair One," the Higher-Up told her.

A red dot appeared on Pennie's prefrontal cortex.

"Fair One LARA B3, you may now leave," Lady Fairship said.

Laraby stood. Pennie glanced over at him but this time when

she moved, intense pain shot through her forehead. "Good bye, Fair One," Laraby said, before turning to the Fairships and bowing. Without another word, he walked out from under the spotlight.

"Laser's ready," the Higher-Up said. "Fair One, please state your identity."

"PENN 1."

The same scene they had all just watched started over again.

7

Fair City

"It appears as though the client has discovered her element."

"I can explain," Pennie said.

Lady Fairship's lips curled into a snarky smile. An image of Tenley Tylwyth blowing away the Frisbee remained frozen on the screen.

"How long has she been aware?" Lord Fairship asked.

The Higher-Up tapped his screen. "It looks as though her first usage was at six months old."

"*Six months*?" Lady Fairship gasped. "The client has known since she was a *baby*?"

"Show us, please." Lord Fairship sat back in his seat.

The screen blipped on again.

A baby sleeps soundly in her crib under a mobile of sparkling fairies. For a moment, nothing happens. But then, the baby rolls onto her side and loses her pacifier. She starts to fret and stir. She locks eyes on the pacifier and blows out a quick breath. The pacifier starts to rock back and forth. Once it builds up enough momentum, the pacifier rolls back into the baby's open mouth. Immediately, the breeze stops and the baby settles back into a deep sleep.

The lights snapped on.

"My goodness, that *is* early," Lord Fairship said.

"It's your *duty* to report early elemental activity, Fair One."

Pennie swallowed. "It could have been the natural wind that moved the pacifier."

"The window was closed, Fair One PENN 1," Lord Fairship pointed out. "Lady Fairship is right. Why didn't you report this?"

Pennie started to argue again, but they'd just seen into her deep memory cortex. There was no use lying. "I should have. Doesn't it make sense, though, that by using their elements early, the clients can better protect themselves?"

Lord Fairship looked disappointed. "Any client that becomes aware of his or her element before they turn eighteen years old is a direct target for Mother Nature. So in fact, by *not* reporting her, you are putting your client in *more* danger."

"*Were*," Lady Fairship said. "You're terminated."

"*What?*" Pennie stood.

"I'm afraid Lady Fairship is correct," Lord Fairship agreed. "You've failed your rookie assignment and there are no second chances. Your client will be scheduled for an immediate erase."

Pennie stepped back, hitting her tiny heel against the leg of the chair. "An erase?"

"Standard procedure." Lady Fairship raised her eyebrow. "Frankly, it should have been done when the client was still a baby. It's a wonder that she's made it this far without being discovered. How long has it been, exactly?" she asked the Higher-Up.

"She's known she possesses the Wind element for twelve and a half years, Lady Fairship."

"Dreadful. As I keep saying," she mumbled to Lord Fairship, "some of these Fair Ones cannot be trusted."

"Not now," Lord Fairship warned her quietly.

"Your Fairships." Pennie swallowed the lump in her throat. "My client has only used her element a few times. So I wouldn't say she *possesses* it, exactly. Her aim isn't always perfect, if you know what I mean." Pennie laughed nervously.

No one else did.

"It is indeed unfortunate that in a situation like this erasing a client's existence is our only option." Lord Fairship clasped his hands. "But you said it yourself; Earth is a dangerous place for the elemental teen. As a thirteen-year-old, your client still has five more years until she no longer requires a Fair One to protect her."

"She'll be safe with me, your Fairship. I promise."

Lord Fairship sat back. "We do not make these decisions lightly. However, we must think of the entire human race first. Your client has powers we need and Mother Nature wants. Should she capture your client, she will absorb her—in this case—wind power and use it against us. Mother Nature has scouts searching day and night for elemental teens like your client and the closer they get to eighteen, the brighter they appear on her radar." He leaned forward. "PENN 1, I think you know that bringing her here for us to immediately erase is a much kinder option that what Mother Nature would do to her."

Pennie looked away. Lord Fairship was right. Stories of what Mother Nature did to the elemental teens were horrific. Absorbing their power was slow and torturous, and no one ever heard from them again. Still, Pennie thought, Tenley Tylwyth had only five more years until she would be officially trained and enlisted in the Elemental Bureau of Fair Force. Five more years! And there was another reason she couldn't let Tenley get erased.

"What about Mrs. Tylwyth?" she asked. "If you take Tenley from her, she'll be devastated."

"You know very well that your client will never even have *existed* for her mother," Lady Fairship said. "Every human who has ever been associated with any client we've had to erase is stripped of all memory of them." She turned to the Higher-Up. "This was an entire *chapter* in the Manual. Put in a request to review all the written Fair One exams."

He clicked on his tablet.

"The decision has been made," Lord Fairship said, smoothing down his beard. "You will be brought to Administration promptly."

"Administration?" Pennie choked.

"Also standard procedure, PENN 1." Lady Fairship smiled.

"Had you turned your client in when you first learned she had discovered her element, you would have been allowed to join the weapons department or cooking staff, or any number of Fair One support systems. Unfortunately, you didn't."

Pennie rushed toward them. "I can't go to Administration. I won't."

In an instant, two Fair Force dropped down and yanked her arms behind her.

Lord and Lady Fairship gathered their robes and stood.

"Please," Pennie cried.

"There's nothing more we can do," Lord Fairship said.

"Actually, there *is* something." Laraby stepped out from the darkened doorway.

One of the Fair Force started toward him until Lord Fairship raised his hand.

"Begging your pardons." Laraby bowed quickly. "There is one thing that Fair One PENN 1 can do to save her client."

"What is it?" Pennie asked.

"Page 300,121, Section 10,008, third paragraph: The Right to Delete. *In which a Fair One is afforded forty-eight hours to convince their client to willingly delete his or her elemental power, thereby rendering an Immediate Erase unnecessary,*" Laraby recited from memory.

Pennie looked from Laraby to the Fairships and back to Laraby. "I'll do it."

Lord Fairship turned to Pennie. "What Fair One LARA B3 is suggesting is a very difficult—"

"And usually unsuccessful—" Lady Fairship added.

"—attempt to get their client to give up their elemental power," Lord Fairship finished.

"Usually unsuccessful?" Pennie glanced at Laraby.

"I'm just citing the rules." He shrugged.

"It requires a complete surrendering," the Higher-Up added.

"A human being does not often volunteer to give up power. Any power. But the power to make the skies rain or the wind blow or lightning strike—well, that's hardly something *any* being wants to give up, particularly a teenage being." Lady Fairship glared at Pennie.

Pennie stood straighter. "I said, I'll do it."

"You should probably think about it," Laraby warned her. "There's a little more to it."

"I said, I'll *do* it," Pennie shouted. "*I'll do it!*"

Lord Fairship nodded to the Higher-Up and gathered his robes once again. "Very well. Fair Force will take you to Room Seventy-one. Good luck, PENN 1."

Lord Fairship disappeared through the wall, and after a last lingering look of contempt, Lady Fairship did the same. The Higher-Up spun away with his tablet, pushed open the door, and disappeared as well.

Pennie shook her head at Laraby. "You've been here the whole time?"

"I've never seen a deep memory laser before. I wanted to watch."

"Thanks, Laraby."

The Fair Force steered her toward the door.

"Don't thank me yet." He stepped out of their way. "It's

true. A Right to Delete is almost always unsuccessful. Which means there's a chance you've just made the worst decision of your life."

"What's worse than becoming an Administrator?" Pennie asked.

"There are a few things," Laraby said.

Pennie was about to ask what those might be, just before the Fair Force pushed her out the door.

8

Hadley Beach

Sylma Tylwyth, short as she was, could only just see over the huge stack of food she pushed in her cart.

Tenley Tylwyth pranced ahead of her mother down the Chips 'n Snacks aisle. Her sash was still draped over her shoulder, "Vote for Me, Tenley T!" on the front and "America's Next Most Inspirational Teen!" on the back.

"I thought we'd have lasagna tonight," Mrs. Tylwyth said, taking the strawberry *Be Awesome* bar that Tenley handed her and balancing it on top of the pile.

"Mom, if I'm going to win the ANMIT nomination, I can't eat lasagna. That's made in like, Italy or somewhere." Tenley plucked a jar of peanut butter off the shelf and handed it to her mother. "I have to eat only American food, remember? That was part of my pledge?"

Mrs. Tylwyth waited for Tenley to giggle.

But Tenley didn't look like she was kidding. In fact, she looked like she was making a mental list. "So. This is what I'm thinking: Double-stuffed baked potatoes, those are like totally American, and sirloin tips and corn on the cob. Then for breakfast, pancakes, maple syrup, and Lucky Charms. All totally American."

"It's not the season for corn on the cob, honey."

Tenley spun around. Mrs. Tylwyth had to swerve the cart not to hit her. A few cereal boxes and a container of marshmallow fluff landed on the floor.

"Anything's possible, Mom, if you want it bad enough. You're the one who told me that." She leaned down to pick up the fallen items. "You're going to be the mother of *America's Next Most Inspirational Teen*." She threw out her hands and pulled her mother in for a hug. "Hopefully."

Mrs. Tylwyth blinked back tears. "You know what, honey? I think we can find some in the frozen food section."

At the checkout line, the tired-looking but pleasant clerk dropped the magazine she was reading and nodded a warm hello. "I'm sorry, ladies, but this is for twelve items."

Tenley pointed at their cart. "We have twelve."

"Or less," the clerk answered. "Aisle three is open."

Aisle three had an old, bent-over cashier and a line four carts deep.

"Well, the thing is, ma'am, I'm trying to get nominated for *America's Next Most Inspirational Teen*."

"Oh, jeez, that's great." The clerk smiled at Mrs. Tylwyth.

"Thank you," Tenley said. "And it's on in, like, fifteen minutes, so I kind of need to get home to watch it."

"You're on TV in fifteen minutes?" The clerk flipped on her conveyer belt. "Well, what are ya' doin here? Let's get you out."

"Oh no—" Mrs. Tylwyth waved. "Tenley, I think you've confused this nice woman. The voting isn't for a few more days."

The clerk stopped rushing and looked up. "Oh."

Tenley grinned. "My mom's right. I'm sorry, I didn't mean to confuse you. I just really, really want to win so I watch every single episode from last year to try to learn as much as I can about how to be the most inspirational teenager that I can be."

The clerk looked impressed. "Well, that's something pretty great, then. What do you do to inspire your fellow teens?" She winked at Mrs. Tylwyth. "I got two of 'em. One's always on her what-not device. And the other's crazy about that *Naked and Not Found* show. Can't get enough of it."

"Nail art," Tenley said proudly. "I think it's super important for girls to feel confident about their hands. I have a nail art tutorial on my YouTube channel."

The clerk stared at Tenley.

"You're very kind," Mrs. Tylwyth pointed to the *Twelve Items or Less* sign.

The clerk looked at Mrs. Tylwyth. "Think nothing of it. You've got yourself a real go-getter here. I'll be rooting for you ..."

Tenley pointed to her sash. "Tenley T. Vote for me!"

At the exit, Mrs. Tylwyth stopped. A rainstorm was flooding the parking lot.

"Oh, dear. I think we should wait it out," Mrs. Tylwyth said.

"I can't, Mom. The show starts in seven minutes."

"It's dangerous to drive in this, Tenley. I'm sorry." Mrs. Tylwyth backed the cart up and disappeared around the corner.

Tenley frowned. When she was sure no one was watching, she ran outside, glanced upwards, and blew. Once. Twice. The rain overhead began to subside. She blew a third time and the clouds broke apart, forming a clearing over the parking lot.

She hurried back inside and found her mother. "Mom, it stopped. Let's go." Tenley grabbed the cart and hurried out the door before Mrs. Tylwyth could protest.

9

Fair City

Room 71 was completely empty.

"Someone will be with you shortly," the Fair Force said before closing the door and leaving Pennie alone.

Pennie stepped in farther. Without her tool belt, the bottoms of her robes were dragging and starting to gray.

A moment later, a very small Fairship stepped directly out of the wall and into the room. "Oh, goody. I heard you were coming." Almost reaching Pennie's shoulders, making her three feet tall at best, the Fairship's white robes had splatters of color across them. They also had red cuffs. She was an Original Eight.

Pennie prepared herself for another cranky tone, but instead this Lady Fairship smiled. "I hope you weren't waiting long."

"Not at all," Pennie said, admiring how the Fairship's curly red hair hung loosely around her face. Pennie checked on her own tight bun.

"I'm Tinktoria. Please call me Tink. And you must be Fair One PENN 1?"

"Yes."

"Follow me." She waved.

Pennie hurried after her, but stopped when Tinktoria disappeared through the wall.

"Oopsie!" she heard Tink say before reappearing again. "I always forget that everyone else needs one of these too." She slipped one of two quartz crystals in the shape of an eight from around her neck and handed it to Pennie. She tucked the other one back under her robes.

"This is beautiful," Pennie said. The crystal was as big as her palm and glowing.

"Let's try this again. Follow me." Tink disappeared once more.

Pennie didn't move.

"Come on now," she called through the wall. "Take a step. You'll see."

Pennie wrapped her fingers around the crystal and stepped forward. Her foot disappeared. She took another step and found herself on the other side of the wall. "*Wow.*"

Assuming Pennie was impressed with walking through the wall, Tink nodded. But it was the explosion of colors Pennie was talking about. Easels and canvases littered the room. Paint splotches covered the floor. She had never seen these colors anywhere in Fair City. With the exception of the Fair Ones' red hair, Fair City was grayscale—differing shades of black until the lightest black became white.

"Now you know what I do in my free time, which, between you and me, is most of the time." Tink waved to the paintings, all of Earth: rivers and forests and oceans. "Oh. Crystal, please."

Pennie dropped the crystal eight back into Tink's hand. "I've never seen so much color in Fair City before."

"Yes, well. We are grossly lacking in it."

Tink led Pennie through the maze of art to a large hammock hanging from the ceiling. Two potted trees sat on either side of it. Built from space junk inside the asteroid belt, Fair City was nothing but bits of rock and debris. Pennie had never seen a tree in person before, but some Fair Ones suspected there were a few hidden in privileged places.

She reached out to touch a leaf, then stopped.

"Oh, go on!" Tink flapped her hand. "Let me introduce you; this is Hap and this is Happier." She smiled at her little palm trees and repositioned the two sun lamps next to them. "Difficult place, Earth. But it does produce some gems."

Pennie stroked the leaves gently. Velvet.

"Now, I was just taking a siesta," Tink said as she dropped into the hammock and patted the spot next to her, "when they told me you'd be dropping by."

Pennie sat gingerly. Tink didn't seem bothered when they collapsed into each other.

"PENN 1. I knew a BENN 1 once. Long time ago. Oh! I forgot the tea. And I forgot to ask, tea?"

"Okay, sure. Thanks," Pennie said.

Tink hopped off the hammock and walked over to a purple square painted on the wall. "Let's get down to business. I'll

47

need to know a few things." After a quick tap on the square, a hologram screen appeared with a photo of Pennie standing very straight with a serious look on her face. Instead of robes, she wore a white shirt and big roomy bloomers.

"This was your official Fair One application photo." Tink pressed another spot on the wall, a green square, and reached in for two mugs of steaming tea.

"I don't even remember taking this." Pennie studied the photo. She looked the same, except for the shorter red hair. Other than that, she had the same small nose, grayish-greenish eyes and full cheeks.

"We keep all Fair One information on Fairbook. Here you are." She handed Pennie one of the mugs and placed her own on a small shelf that appeared on the wall as soon as she walked by it. "Now, I understand your client is to be erased?"

A hologram tablet, having appeared on the shelf next to the tea, started calculating something.

"No," Pennie said. "That's why I'm here."

"Of course. You're interested in The Right to Delete. Forty-eight hours to convince your client to delete her elemental power, which is ..."

"Wind."

"That's a good one. Not the best, but good. Personally, I'd want the water element. Water is life, after all. But you get what you get, I suppose."

Pennie smiled politely. Ever since the Super's disappearance, some humans were born with weather powers. No one knew why. But once the Fairships realized these humans were in

48

more danger than the average human, the original Protection Plan was rewritten to give each one of these clients their own Fair One.

"Now," Tink said. "This *challenge* you are entering into is a little *dicey*. We have to make sure you understand this."

Pennie looked at the corners of the ceiling. "Are we being recorded?"

"What *isn't* being recorded in Fair City?" Tink clicked on the tablet. "Six months old when she discovered her element?"

"I know I should have reported it. But I was afraid of what you, I mean not *you* you, but what the Fair Force would do to her."

"Exactly what they will do to her if she doesn't agree to give up her element in forty-eight hours."

Pennie looked stricken.

Tink realized her curtness. "I apologize, Fair One. It seems you care about your client a great deal." She softened. "Why?"

"She's my client. It's my job."

"Yes, exactly. It's *just* a job. And if it's proving too dangerous to keep your client where she is, then it's your job to hand her over to us."

Pennie squirmed in the hammock.

"What is it, Fair One? If there's a skeleton in your closet, best to get it out now. I can find everything I need to know in our database anyway."

Pennie hesitated. She'd never told this to anyone. "One day, when Tenley Tylwyth was about two years old, I wasn't observing her as closely as I should have been." Pennie struggled with her words. "I went on an unauthorized space trip. Anyway, my client must have been practicing her wind element because right when I got back to the ob-spot, the palm tree next to their house was swaying out of control. Violently. I tried to stop it, but I was too late. Skipper Tylwyth, Tenley's father, was only inches away from it when it fell into their living room."

"Her element had that much force at such a young age?"

Pennie nodded. "The thing is, after narrowly escaping death, he vowed never to live anywhere near palm trees, or any other trees, again."

"Are you saying her father left?"

"A fishing rig. In Alaska. He's never come back." Pennie felt a sting in her heart.

"And still, even after that, you refused to report your client?"

"It was *my* fault. I should have stopped that tree from falling. I could have if I hadn't gone with my friends." Pennie looked down.

"I see. And your client," Tink swiped at the tablet, "she's interested in winning a beauty contest?"

Pennie tried to sit higher in the hammock, but slid back down again. "*America's Next Most Inspirational Teen,* actually."

"How serious is she about winning?"

"Very. Local nominations are in two days. If she wins that, she goes onto the national level." Pennie lowered her voice. "I think she's determined to get famous so her father will see her on TV."

Tink looked suspicious. "Determined enough to use her element for the talent portion of this contest?"

"No. No way. She'd never do that." But Pennie's stomach flipped. If Tenley used her element on TV, Mother Nature would find her in an instant.

Tink looked unconvinced. "Let's get you ready." She took the tea from her, still untouched.

"My tool belt is checked at the front."

"You won't be needing that."

"Great." Fair Force technology was infinitely more advanced than Fair One tools. Monitoring a client through a 3rdi-All was rumored to feel so much like standing on Earth that some Fair Force got queasy.

After struggling with the hammock, Pennie followed Tink past the canvases and paint, and back to the wall again. Tink handed Pennie the crystal eight, and once they were on the other side, Pennie handed it back to her.

"All clear," Tink said stepping into the hallway. "Quickly now."

Tink moved fast on her tiny feet. After a few twists and turns, the two stopped in front of a break in the wall.

"We try not to be obvious about where Command Center is," Tink whispered at Pennie's confused look. "Never can be too careful."

"The *real* Command Center?"

"It's the only access point, my dear."

"To where?"

Tink stepped inside the door. "Earth."

Pennie froze. Earth was the last place a Fair One wanted to go.

10

Hadley Beach

Mrs. Tylwyth stepped out the door. Tenley's backpack was slung over one arm. She juggled a poster board, Scotch tape, two bags of confetti, and a stack of streamers with the other.

"Mom, I need dry erase markers, too!" Tenley yelled from the upstairs window. "Can we go get some?"

"I'm sorry, honey. I have to get the store open early today for a delivery. Mrs. Frontalbagger died last week and her son is bringing me all her furniture."

Tenley closed the window. Mrs. Tylwyth balanced her piles carefully and opened the back door of their car. A roll of pink streamers dropped to the ground and began unraveling down the driveway. She leaned over to grab it and another roll dropped.

Tenley walked outside brushing her hair, leaving the front door wide open as usual. She headed for the driver's side. "I'm driving, Mom. K?"

Mrs. Tylwyth threw the rest of the pile into the car.

"I don't think today is the best day for you to start driving," she said. "It looks like it might rain and there was a report on the news this morning about a sudden flash flood that flipped a car right over onto its side. A flash flood! Out of nowhere! Besides, it's Waffle Day. You don't want to be late for that."

"Please, Mom? How can I pass the test if I've never even practiced? I only have three years until I take it. All the contestants on ANMIT are expected to pass on their first try."

"Such crazy weather lately," Mrs. Tylwyth mumbled to herself. "It's like Mother Nature's out to get us. Plus, Tenley, it's illegal for you to drive." She gathered up the streamers and threw this mess into the car, too.

"Just to the end of the driveway?" Tenley smiled sweetly.

Mrs. Tylwyth folded. She looked at her watch, sighed heavily, and walked around to the passenger door where she slid into their small, practical car. Tenley hurried to the driver's side and climbed in.

Tenley moved the rearview mirror around to frame her face. She smoothed down her hair and puckered her lips to check on her lip liner. Then she opened her window and closed it again. She took off her shoes and threw them into the backseat. She fiddled with the radio, which wasn't even on.

"You could be there by now," Mrs. Tylwyth said.

Tenley started the car. Mrs. Tylwyth cringed. Tenley gave her a quick smile, turned her head to back out, and drove straight into the garage.

The door dented like a piece of toast.

"Tenley!" Mrs. Tylwyth threw her arms up. "I just had that fixed again."

Tenley stepped out of the car, walked to the passenger side, and opened the door. "I'm sorry, Mom. I did really well until the door part, though."

A few minutes later, Mrs. Tylwyth stopped in front of the school and scribbled on Tenley's outstretched palm. Tenley stepped out, opened the back door, and grabbed her backpack. Then she took her sash, slung it over her head, and secured it at her hip. She thanked her mom, slammed the door, and turned for school.

Just inside the building, Mr. Frimpy's figure loomed large, as usual. But today there was somebody next to him. Somebody tall, dark, and hot.

"Thanks for coming, son," Mr. Frimpy, substantially smaller than the hot guy standing next to him, said. "The gym is all set for the auditions right after third period."

"I sure appreciate it, Principal Frimpy."

The hottie shook the principal's hand and spun around directly into Tenley. "Oops. Sorry."

"Cheer auditions?" Tenley asked with a bright smile. "Omigod wait!" She grabbed Mr. Frimpy's arm. "Is Hadley Middle School holding an *America's Next Most Inspirational Teen* nomination audition?" She bounced on her toes. "That's so much better than the Community Center. You won't be sorry, Mr. Frimpy. I'll make you proud. I'll make the whole school proud!"

"No, Ms. Tylwyth." Mr. Frimpy pulled his arm out of Tenley's clutch. "We're not holding ANMIT auditions."

She stopped bouncing. "Oh. Well for the record, I think we should." She shifted her body so the hot guy could read her sash. "Are you an ANMIT scout?"

Mr. Frimpy sighed. He'd have to introduce them now. "This is Dan Ringer. He's a new senior over at Hadley High School and he's volunteered to run the auditions here. Lucky for all of us, his father was asked to relocate." Big smile.

"Hello," Dan said.

"Hello. So, are your auditions open to anyone?" Tenley asked.

Dan nodded. "Sure, yeah. As long as you come prepared, we're expecting some stiff competition."

"G.R.E.A.T!" Tenley cheered, kicking her leg, barely missing Mr. Frimpy.

Mr. Frimpy cleared his throat. "Miss Tylwyth, this is your twenty-ninth tardy so far this school year."

"Yes, Mr. Frimpy," Tenley said. "My mom is so sorry. She lost her keys and we had to tear apart the house looking for them and then she drove right into the garage door. Again. It's like the *millionth* time she's done that. Boy, is my dad gonna be mad. And she told me to tell you to drop by the antique store anytime. New shipment today."

"Note?"

"Right here." Tenley held out her palm. *Sorry Tenley is late again car accident my fault, Sylma Tylwyth* was written in black ink. Mr. Frimpy'd seen enough of the handwriting to know it was, indeed, Mrs. Tylwyth's. "Please don't be mad at her, Mr. Frimpy. You know she's a really bad driver."

"Next time get it on paper."

"Sure thing." Tenley pranced down the empty hallway, certain Dan was watching.

11

Fair City

"I can't go to *Earth*."

Tink smiled at Pennie. "How else do you think you're going to get your client to give up her element? Certainly not from up here?"

Command Center was dense with Fair Force in compact cubicles. Most of their screens were monitoring important sites: the Statue of Liberty, the Golden Gate Bridge, Mount Rushmore. A few other screens seemed to be tracking individuals, while a few more were tracking large crowds.

Tink led Pennie through another doorway to a center stage where hundreds of screens floated in and out of each other. These Fair Force sat in front of 3D hologram screens so clear that Pennie stepped over non-existent rocks and shielded her eyes from rainfall.

"Command Center!" Tink shouted over the noise. "Inner sanctum."

Tink led Pennie toward two empty keyboards in a back corner. There, she sat on what looked to be nothing but air. Pennie hesitated but Tink patted the empty space next to her. "It's an iWind seat. They're fabulous."

Pennie squealed when the invisible force caught her. "I never knew we had these."

"*You* don't. Everything in here is classified Fair Force equipment." Tink slid on a headset. "Now. What did you say the client's address was?"

"Nineteen Nathan Lane. Hadley Beach."

"And where's that?"

"California."

"California," Tink repeated, entering the information.

A screen materialized in front of them and an image of Earth began zooming in. Tink placed a flat hand on her stomach. "That gets me every time. You wouldn't happen to know the zip code?"

"90266."

Tink entered the numbers and the image zoomed closer, into the United States, to the West Coast, to Los Angeles County, and eventually to Hadley Beach and 19 Nathan Lane.

"That's a much better image than we get. What are you using?"

"It's classified Fair Force technology. They're working on an updated visual for you, I've heard."

"A 3rdi-All?" Pennie asked hopefully.

"I'm afraid not. That's still only Lieutenant Fair One equipment. Now, let's see where we are." Tink studied the screen.

"It's like I'm actually *standing* in their driveway. There *has* to be a way I can do the Right to Delete from here."

"There isn't," Tinktoria said. "She'll need to sign this."

Tink tapped her temple and a hologram form letter materialized in front of them.

"*I hereby agree to cease and desist all use of my personal elemental power until further notice or forever, whichever comes first.*" Pennie read. "Really? That's all she needs to do. Sign this?"

"That's it." Tink flicked her hand, making the hologram disappear.

Pennie sighed, relieved. "So in general, like in past Right to Deletes, do they just sign it when the Fair One shows up with it?"

"There are a few other stipulations. You'll have to read the fine print."

"There's fine print?"

"There's always fine print, Fair One. It's in your Intel. RTD Form 0100." Tink tapped her temple again.

Another hologram form appeared. Pennie stepped closer to it and squinted. It was very, *very* fine.

"Basically," Tink said. "It says something along the lines of: *Once the form has been signed, any further use of the four elements—wind, water, lightning, fire—by the client will result in an Immediate Erase of client and Banishment of Fair One. Any*

59

injuries caused by such arrest shall be neither the fault nor the responsibility of Fair Force LLC ... and so on."

"Wa—wa—wait. No one said anything about the Fair One getting *banished*."

"Yes they did. Right here. In the fine print."

"If my client signs the form, but then accidentally conjures up a small breeze—"

"You're both goners." Tink nodded. "One way or the other."

Pennie tried to register this. Banishment was to be sent off into deep space. Alone. Forever. Never to be heard from again.

"You're looking a little peaked. Still want to go through with it?"

"Of course. Yeah. *Yes.*"

"All right then." Tink waved the hologram away.

"Just one thing. How exactly do I explain everything to my client, starting with the fact that she's been born with a weather element and is in constant danger of being discovered by Mother Nature?"

"Reason with her."

"She's a *teenager*."

"I see your point. It's a tough age for that. I recall a few Fair Ones trying some sort of cattle shocking device. I don't have one of those to give to you, though. They managed to get hold of them on their own."

"What happens if I *do* succeed? Do I get reassigned to a new client?"

"Honestly, I'm not quite sure. I don't remember anyone succeeding before. Of course, I've only been in this department for eight decades."

"No one's succeeded in *eighty years*?"

"A Right to Delete is extremely difficult to accomplish. It was only created to appease the Unions, which is why it's in the very, very, *very* fine print of the *Official Manual*. You must have an expert knowledge of the rules to even know about it."

Laraby. Pennie groaned. He was right—she shouldn't have thanked him yet. "If it's this hard, why am I bothering to try at all?"

"I don't know, Fair One. Why are you?"

Pennie looked back at the Tylwyth house on the screen. How could she live with herself if she didn't at least *try* to save Tenley? Besides, being a miserable Administrator was no way to live.

But going to Earth? She couldn't.

She turned to Tink and shook her head. "I'd do anything to save her except go to Earth."

"That's good to know." Tink stood and started for the exit.

"So what do we do next?" Pennie hurried after her.

"I have my art to get back to. I'm sure you have some things to take care of before you're sent to Administration."

Pennie stopped. "Isn't there a plan B?"

Tink turned around. "My dear Fair One. You have been given this forty-eight hour period to prove *us* wrong, not the other way around. We've made our decision." Tink took her hand. "I know you're worried for your client, Fair One. I assure you, though, getting erased is painless and a much kinder alternative than getting taken by Mother Nature. You're doing the right thing. As for Administration, it's not as terrible as they say. You might even enjoy it." Tink dropped Pennie's hand and started for the exit.

"Enjoy it?" Pennie repeated. "Wait. Please!" Pennie grabbed the red cuff on Tink's long sleeve.

Tink glared at her.

"Sorry," Pennie dropped it. "I'll go."

Tink considered her. "Is this your final answer?"

"Yes."

"Fine." Tink reversed toward the monitoring station. Pennie caught a look at one of the screens as she passed it; massive clouds were colliding somewhere and the Fair Force in the room were laser focused on it.

"I'll be right back," Tink said before disappearing into the wall.

Pennie walked closer to the monitors. Whatever was brewing in the skies above Earth looked sinister.

Tink reappeared. "The only thing you need to take with you is this time device."

"A watch?"

"You're familiar with them?"

"Sure. Is that a dinosaur?"

There was a purple dinosaur in the center.

"We can't send you down with any of our technology in case it gets into the wrong hands." Tink handed Pennie the watch. "So we copied some of the watches we've seen the clients wear."

"Really *young* clients, you mean. A toddler maybe?"

Tink brushed away the idea. "It's programmed on stopwatch

mode for forty-eight hours and will begin at eight a.m. Earth time."

A large clock on the wall displayed: EARTH TIME 7:58 a.m.

"That's in *two* minutes!"

Tink continued, unfazed. "The Fair Force will arrive at the forty-eight hour mark. If your client has signed the form by then, she will be taken into temporary custody where her element will be properly deleted. After which, she will be returned to her regular, *un*-elemented life on Earth. She'll be just a regular kid with no recollection of ever being able to create wind."

Pennie nodded.

"If she has *not* signed the form by then," Tink eyes softened. "Well, you know."

Pennie slipped on the stopwatch.

"Where are my instructions?"

"No instructions." Tink smoothed down some of her loose red hair.

Pennie blinked at her. "What about clothes?"

"We don't have access to their wardrobes. You'll have to figure that out when you get there."

Pennie shook her head. "That's it? That's all you have to tell me?"

"There is one more thing. The stopwatch will buzz sixty minutes before the forty-eight-hour time period is up. And it will do so again at the ten-minute, three-minute, and thirty-second mark. You and your client should be as far away from anyone else as possible when the Fair Force arrives so fewer memories will need to be erased."

The clock on the wall read: EARTH TIME 7:59 a.m.

Tink pulled the crystal eight off from around her neck and pushed open a door. Behind it was a set of elevator doors. "This is the travel box. Once you step inside, the temporary disintegration will begin. You'll need to stay completely still during this process. When the doors open again, you should be at nineteen Nathan Lane, or somewhere around there, anyway."

Pennie's mouth went dry. This was ridiculous. No instructions, no tools, no pants.

Tink slipped the crystal eight directly into the elevator doors and turned it like a key. As soon as the travel box opened, she ushered Pennie in.

"Earth is a perfectly safe place to be, once gravity is dealt with. Although it is rather hard to stay awake down there. I've heard of entire trips spent *sleeping*. Imagine that journey and then never even waking up!" She pointed to the ceiling. "Just remember to stand directly under the laser and stay as still as you can. You'll want to arrive in one piece."

"*Code Red. Repeat: We have a Code Red. Irregular activity spotted. Renegade Weathers suspected. All Force in the area to respond immediately.*"

An alarm drowned out Tink's next words.

"What's happening?" Pennie shouted. The doors were shutting.

"Security Breach. You better get going before they suspend all travel. Good luck!"

The doors closed.

The stopwatch beeped on.

12

48:00:00
Fair City

Inside the travel box, a thick beam of light flickered above Pennie's head. Her fingers and toes started to tingle. The sensation slid up her arms and down her legs. She gritted her teeth, trying not to move. The travel box began to shake and the laser burned hotter. Pennie's head felt like it might explode. She stifled a scream and then ...

The laser blacked out.

The elevator doors broke apart.

Command Center was in chaos. Hologram monitors were blinking and Fair Force were scrambling toward the exit. Everywhere, floors were cracking and walls were crumbling.

Pennie rushed through the elevator doors. "Tink?" she yelled. But Tink was nowhere to be seen.

The stopwatch read **47:59:20.** She inspected it closer. There was no pause button. The floor below her rumbled and buckled. She jumped off just before it cracked open. A meter away, she spotted something glowing under a pile of debris.

Tink's crystal eight.

"Tink!" Pennie yelled, swiping it up. "Tinktoria, are you in here?"

There was no answer and she couldn't be heard over the alarm anyway. She slid the crystal eight into her pocket. The wall in front of her crumbled. The exit was blocked.

Pennie fought her way over to center stage where Fair Force were shouting orders at the largest screen. It was a live picture of a building on fire. Surrounding it, trees toppled and roads buckled. Cars sped out of control and everywhere, people were running, covered in dust. Pennie was witnessing an earthquake.

"Has anyone seen Tinktoria?" she yelled.

"*Contact initiated,*" a computer-generated voice sounded over the loudspeaker.

The center screen changed to a busy city sidewalk with a group of businessmen and women walking together. They all popped in earbuds without breaking their stride. "We can hear you, Commander. Go on," one of the businessmen said.

"Very good," the commander yelled. "We are seeing heavy fire in an occupied building. We need your group of elementals to deploy to 34.0500 degrees South 118.2500 degrees West immediately. We believe we are having simultaneous attacks both here and in Southern California."

"We're on our way, Commander," the businessman said.

The floor below Pennie gave way. She grabbed onto a wall.

On screen, the elementals slipped left down a side street and huddled together. A moment later, they lifted off from the cement. Without propellers. Which meant someone in that group had the wind element. That would have been Tenley someday, Pennie couldn't help thinking. But now she'd be lucky just to stay on Earth, alive. *If* Pennie could get to her in time.

Pennie checked the stopwatch. **47:57:50**. She banged on the dinosaur face. "Stop already!" It didn't.

Pennie made her way over to a Fair Force stationed in front of his keyboard.

"Excuse me, can you help me with that?" She pointed back to the travel box.

The Fair Force scowled. "It's Code Red. All travel is suspended."

"Where's Tink?"

"Who?"

"Tinktoria," she shouted. "From Room Seventy-one?"

"Not my department."

Pennie lifted the stopwatch to him. "Could you stop it, please?"

He shook his head. "Don't handle Fair One equipment."

"But this is an emergency!"

The keyboard in front of the Fair Force exploded. He flew sideways and directly into Pennie. Before she knew what had happened, she felt herself falling through the floor.

13

47:50:01
Earth

"What was that?" A girl panicked at the sink.

"It felt like an earthquake," a voice answered from one of the stalls.

"I'm getting out of here," the girl said, turning off the water and sprinting for the door.

Unfazed, Tenley picked up the lipstick that she'd dropped and watched the girl go. She smacked her lips and smiled at herself. Then she pushed open the girl's bathroom door and—*slam*!

"Ow." Holden Wonderbolt grabbed his head.

Tenley flipped her hair. "Sorry. No pictures."

"What?"

"Well, okay, one." Tenley froze in a fierce pose.

Holden stared at her. Then checked behind him. No one

taking pictures anywhere.

"Hey, you've got a thing?"

Tenley pointed to her sash. *"Vote for Me, Tenley T.* I'm trying ... ugh *stop it Tenley!"* She gave herself a mental shake. *"Positive* thinking, *positive* thinking." She stood straighter and smiled. "I'm *going* to get nominated for America's Next Most Inspirational Teen."

"No, I mean—" Holden pointed down. "You've got a situation there."

Tenley looked at the toilet paper stuck to her beige flats.

"Oh." Mortified, she scraped her foot off on a nearby trash bin and waved. "Thank you, voter."

"Yeah. No problem," Holden called after her. "Hey! Was everything okay yesterday? After that Frisbee almost hit you? No bruises or anything? Because I—" He raised his blue cast but Tenley was already halfway down the hall. "Got this."

The bell rang and Tenley disappeared into the crowded cafeteria. Not even the smell of syrup was cheering Holden up today.

"What's the face, Wonderbolt? It's Waffle Day!" Someone slapped him on the back.

"Hey, Coach Bleaker." Holden jogged to keep up with him. "You think I'll be okay by play-offs?"

Coach Bleaker noticed his cast. "Geez, I don't know, Wonderbolt. In a week? I'm not a doc, but I'm pretty sure it takes six weeks for bones to heal."

Holden's face fell. He dropped back a few paces.

"But," Coach Bleaker said, turning into the cafeteria, "tell you what. I could use some help on the sidelines. They don't pay me enough to be the assistant coach, too."

Coach Bleaker headed over to the faculty table. Holden stepped into the waffle line. Tenley was four students up in the same line, behind a small redhead.

A boy in front of the redhead stepped back and landed on her foot.

"Ow," the redhead yelped.

"Omigod." Tenley hurried over and pulled the girl into a hug. "Are you okay, ginger?"

"Yeah?"

"You don't look like it." Tenley straightened her sash and prepared for battle. "Hey! Football player guy. Did you just attack this ginger's lower body?"

"Um, no," the boy answered with a frown.

Tenley stepped closer to him. "Did you or did you *not* just step on her foot?"

"I dunno. Maybe, I guess."

"Maybe? Look at this ginger's face. Look how sad it is!"

"It's Andrea. And I'm fine," the girl whispered.

"You don't have to pretend with me, ginger."

The boy, definitely a football player, shook his head and moved forward in the line.

"Wait a minute," Tenley said. "What's your name?"

"Ah, Collin?"

"Everyone? Can I have your attention please?" A few of the students looked up from their tables. Tenley pointed to her sash. "Tenley Tylwyth, running for America's Next Most Inspirational

Teen. As most of you know, I'm running my campaign on the confidence-building effects of nail art. But I've also just, right now, witnessed a real life injustice with this ginger-crusher."

Andrea and Collin exchanged nervous glances.

Tenley slipped her arm around the girl. "You don't need to be afraid, ginger victim."

Collin shook his head. "Hey, I just stepped on Andrea's foot—"

Tenley glared at him. "Gingers are people too! They have feet that can be stepped on just like the rest of us!"

The teachers were starting to notice them.

Collin abandoned his tray and walked out. Three girls in cheerleading outfits stared at her and whispered to each other.

"Really, I'm fine," Andrea said. "Collin's my brother's friend."

Tenley took both of Andrea's shoulders in her hands and shook them. "You have been *far too* brave for *far too* long, ginger. I want you to know that you can count on me, Tenley T. Even when no one else will 'like' your Instagrams or sit with you. Or share your hairbrushes. I will. I am Ginger Strong. And if you nominate me," Tenley smiled to those students still watching. "If *all* of you nominate me as your Hadley Beach representative for ANMIT, I promise I will personally guide the gingers. I will teach them what nail colors they can and cannot wear. I will be their Ginger Ninja." She looked at Andrea. "Sound good, ginger?"

"Andrea."

"You're welcome." Tenley looked back over to the cheerleaders. "Now if you'll excuse me, I have a phone call to make." She spun around and hurried out the door.

14

47:36:20
Fair City

Pennie landed on the floor of the Great Hall. No one even noticed. She picked herself up and brushed down her abundant robes. For once, she was glad to have all the extra padding.

The Great Hall was at a standstill. Administrators and Fair Ones were glued to a giant screen where the same building Pennie had seen in Command Center continued to burn. Everyone cheered when—out of nowhere—dark rain clouds floated across the blue sky and hovered above the building. Heavy rain poured down on it. The fire went out.

"Mama N is angry today!" a Fair One whistled.

Pennie tapped him on the shoulder. "Excuse me. Do you know how to get to Command Center?"

The Fair One looked at her suspiciously. "No. And if you're

trying to get me to admit to something, I didn't do it and I ain't guilty of it neither."

"Right. Okay, is there an escalator around here, maybe?"

The Fair One had already disappeared into the crowd.

Pennie stood on her toes and saw someone she knew— Laraby, walking to the exit.

"Laraby!" She waved.

She rushed through a hologram banner and picked her way around white robes until she came to the Tool Belt Check. The checkout girl was gone. So was Laraby. Pennie searched inside her pocket for the ticket, but it was gone too. Tink's crystal eight was still there though, so she slipped the chain around her neck and tucked it under her robes.

Making sure no one was looking, she ran behind the counter. There were rows of lockers and no way of knowing which one had her tool belt in it. The sound of a nearby explosion shook the ground. Muffled cries came from the hall.

"She's attacking City Hall!" a Fair One shouted, running past the counter and out the door. Pennie followed.

Laraby was halfway down the stairs.

"Laraby!"

He stopped, not looking too happy about it, or to be seeing Pennie.

"You're still here." She ran down to him.

"So are you."

"What's happening? How can *we* be getting attacked?"

"I doubt we are. Could be a crack in the ozone. The effects of the earthquake might be leaking upward. If she was attacking us directly, it would be bigger than a few rumbles." Laraby started down the stairs again.

Pennie continued after him. "There were explosions in Command Center."

Laraby stopped. "You were in Command Center?"

Pennie nodded.

"Did you see their equipment? Their 3rdi-Alls?"

"They have so many amazing tools. *Wind seats*, even." Pennie held out her wrist. "This is official Fair Force equipment. It's counting down the forty-eight hours for The Right to Delete."

Laraby frowned at it.

"I know. They want it to look like human technology. Tinktoria in Room Seventy-one started it, but travel's been suspended. Do you know how to stop it?"

"I'm not privy to Fair Force equipment because I am not yet a Lieutenant Fair One. And the last time I was with you, my chances of becoming one greatly decreased. So if you'll excuse me." He turned back for the stairs. His red beard blew over his shoulder.

"Wait!" Pennie followed after him. "I thought you were that guy?"

"What guy?"

"That guy who knows everything. The guy who knows all the rules."

Laraby stopped. "As a matter of fact, I do know all the rules. What is it you want to know?"

"How to turn this off." She held out her wrist again.

Laraby took a closer look. "I can't help you," he said, starting back down the stairs.

74

"Do you know another way I can get to Earth?"

"Even if I *did* know how to get you there, it's not something you want to do on your own, without Fair Force protection. A myriad of nasty things could snap you up in a nano-second."

From the middle of the staircase, the old disheveled Fair One with the *Bladeless* sign clucked. "Snap you up."

Laraby ignored him.

"We *all* took an oath, Laraby. To protect them. What if it was *your* client?"

"It wouldn't *be* my client. *I* would have reported her right away."

Pennie slumped down on a stair. Laraby turned around.

"I'm sorry, Fair One, but you brought this problem on yourself. You should never have allowed your client to continue using her element. The rules were created for a reason. So right now, breaking another one might not be in your best interest."

"I *knew* it." Pennie stood. "You *do* know a way."

"I didn't say that. I never said that."

"You said *another one*. Another rule. A rule I would need to break to get down there. Please, Laraby, what is it?"

The old Fair One mumbled something.

Laraby started down the stairs again. "No."

Pennie crossed her arms. "Actually, you know what *I* think? I think you don't *know* the rules as well as you *think* you do. So I'll go find someone who does."

Laraby wanted to ignore her. He really did. But no one knew the rules better than he did. No one.

"sipLips!"

Pennie looked over at the old Fair One. "sipLips?"

Laraby stopped.

The old Fair One nodded furiously. "Yes. sipLips. They'll take you down, for something nice."

Pennie glared at Laraby. "Tell me how to find a sipLip."

"It's illegal."

"Tell me how to find a sipLip," she said louder.

Laraby took a step up. "Quiet, will you? Just talking about them can get you reviewed."

"How do I find a sipLip?" Pennie yelled.

Laraby sighed. "Come with me." He pulled a face at the old Fair One before turning away. Pennie hurried after him.

The streets were deserted as far as Pennie could see. She followed Laraby around a corner.

"All right," he stopped. "The sipLips can get you down, but that old Fair One's right. You'll need to give them something for it, like some tools."

"Mine are still locked up." Pennie noticed for the first time that Laraby had his. "That teen Administrator was gone. How did you get yours back?"

"I wired them with voice command."

"Huh?"

"Rule 345632. Fair Ones may add voice command to tool belts for cases of emergency." He shrugged. "So I ordered the handy tool to unlock the lock from inside the locker."

There was no time to be impressed. "Can I give the sipLips one of yours?"

"What? *No.* Do you know how much volunteer work and

76

overtime I've had to do to get all these?" Laraby displayed his tools proudly. Pennie had never seen so many devices on a single Fair One. "I even have the frozen yogurt maker." He pulled out a small metal device in the shape of a cone. "Makes delicious non-fat froyo with a push of a button."

Pennie checked her stopwatch.

"Extravagant, I know. But I've had every standard Fair One tool since my first day on the job. I'd trade them all in for a 3rdi-All, though. Continuous uninterrupted surround sound while retaining a perfect visual, regardless of the client's speed. Imagine. No more losing audio contact when my client gets on his skateboard."

"I hope you get one," Pennie said quietly. Her lower lip trembled.

"Oh no. No crying. Look, PENN 1—"

"Pennie."

"Pennie. I'm sorry I can't help you."

"It was a *rule* from the *Manual*, Laraby. The oath we took? I have to do everything I can to protect my client and that means protecting her from getting erased too."

Laraby paused. She had a point.

"Fine. Follow me," he said, activating his propellers and lifting a few feet off the ground.

Pennie, who had none, was forced to jog next to him instead.

"Where are we going?"

"You'll see."

The air was starting to smell putrid. This was a side of Fair City that no one ever saw and now Pennie wished she hadn't either. The sky used to be a clear gray all over, but lately it was becoming increasingly dark. And here, the sky was nearly black.

Pennie looked at her watch. **47:30:04**. "I've. Already. Lost. Half. An. Hour," she panted. Jogging was not something a Fair One and her tiny feet should do.

A sudden gust of wind blew the dusty soot off the ground and into a frenzy. When the air settled, a *Barely There* diet bar wrapper swirled in and out of Laraby's blades. He pointed to a sign ahead.

The Fair City Dump.

"The dump?"

"*Shh!*" Laraby scolded her, landing perfectly and retracting his propellers.

When they reached the sign, the dump was full of trash but otherwise empty.

"Is anyone here?"

Laraby took something out of his tool belt: the froyo maker.

"Really? You're going to make frozen yogurt *now*?"

"They'll *come* for the froyo."

"Seriously?"

"sipLips can't stay away from it." He placed the froyo maker on the ground. "At least these sipLips can't." Laraby pulled out a flashlight. A green beam of light hit the small metal cone. There was a tiny puff followed by a white container.

Laraby picked up the pint and propelled himself over the first pile of garbage. He flipped the lid off and balanced the container on top of the trash.

"It's better if I'm not here," he said, propelling back to Pennie.

"Are they dangerous?"

"Let's just say I have a history with them … but they won't bother you. And here, if they whine about how that's not enough, offer them an earpiece, too. I've got a few more where those came from."

Pennie took the earpiece and slipped it inside her robes. "How long do you think I'll have to wait?"

"They're on their own time, so who knows. Good luck, Fair One Pennie. If you do get to Earth, remember to breathe. The more oxygen you take in, the faster you'll acclimate and the less you'll need to sleep. Which, by the way, is all you're going to want to do. It's brutal, that gravity."

"Thanks, Laraby."

"Don't thank me yet," he warned, tipping his head to the left and zooming away. "You might be making the biggest mistake of your life."

Pennie watched him go, really wishing he hadn't said that. Again.

15

46:20:07
Hadley Beach

Mrs. Tylwyth stepped into Tenley's room. "Actually, it's a good thing you called. I forgot my catalogues anyway. Have you seen them anywhere?"

"You mean these?" Tenley looked up from the other side of the bed. Two pom-poms made of shredded paper were clutched in her hands. She clapped them together.

"*Tenley*. You said you had to come home because you ate a bad waffle." Mrs. Tylwyth crossed her arms and frowned. "I left the store halfway open."

"I'm sorry, Mom. But I didn't think you'd let me come home if I told you the truth."

"Which is?" Mrs. Tylwyth smoothed down the end of Tenley's bedding before she sat.

"Cheerleading auditions. They're today and I needed pom-

poms. I didn't want you to have to go buy me some real ones, so I made these. I might even use them in my nail tutorials."

"Cheerleading? Why would they be holding auditions at the end of the school year?"

It *was* a little weird, considering it was June. "All I know is that this really cute guy was setting up auditions with Mr. Frimpy and told me I could audition too. Anyway, it's the perfect place to get more votes."

"Honey," Mrs. Tylwyth started.

"Don't *worry*, Mom," Tenley brushed out a pom-pom. "I'm going to get it."

"This is a small town, Tenley. These teens that you're watching, the ones that actually get onto the show and win the nominations, they're from big cities. ANMIT only takes one teen from each state. And these kids have moms and dads who work in big companies where they can get lots of votes, not at their own antique shop. I might only get one or two walk-ins a day, honey, and even though I put your signs up, well, I just don't want you to be heartbroken."

"I'm not going to be heartbroken; I'm going to be nominated." Tenley clapped her pom-poms and stood. "I made these out of your *Secret Antique Finds* catalogues. I mean, am I inspirational or *what*?"

"A paper tutu, too?" Mrs. Tylwyth chuckled.

Tenley swiveled her hips. "Cool, huh?"

"How did you know how to make all that?"

"YouTube, Mom. DIY."

Mrs. Tylwyth couldn't help but look impressed.

81

"So you're not mad at me?"

"No, I'm still mad, Tenley. And you'll have to pay me back for those catalogues. But you are pretty clever."

"Can you take me back to school now please?"

"Let's go." Mrs. Tylwyth walked to the door. "I hope this rain stops soon or I'm afraid you'll be wearing a soggy ball of paper for a tutu."

"It won't rain on us," Tenley said glancing out the window confidently. "I promise."

16

46:00:00
Fair City

Time had not been good to the sipLips. After the Super's disappearance, these descendants of fairies refused to take part in the plan to protect the clients. They felt that their ancestors had been forced into servitude—granting all those wishes and throwing all that pixy dust—long enough. And now, with the Super gone, these fairies had the chance to become something else entirely.

That something else was filthy and rude. And sipping and slurping. They became known as "sipLips."

Fair Ones were heavily discouraged from interacting with sipLips. With no allegiance to either Fairships or Mother Nature, they were out to protect only themselves. After dissolving into a ragtag, unorganized bunch of beings, sipLips became the scavengers of the asteroid belt, willing to do anything for anyone as long as they were rewarded in return—usually with food, sometimes with shelter, and almost always with tools. It was rumored that Mother Nature didn't trust the sipLips any more than the Fairships did. Luckily, with no equipment to call their own and no Weathers to employ, the sipLips were not considered an immediate threat. They *were*, however, alarmingly unappealing.

Pennie stepped back as four of these creatures straightened themselves out in front of her, which made no difference to their appearance. They were filthy. One sipLip had filled the rips in his grimy robes with newspaper. All of them had tool belts around their waists, but only the largest of the sipLips had any tools in it. And their propellers! Rusted and bent and missing blades.

"Howdy-do, Fairly One. You rang?" the largest sipLip asked with a sloppy smile. His teeth, the ones that remained, were the same color as his robes.

Pennie's trembling voice was so far inside her throat she had trouble getting the words out. "My friend did, yes."

He studied Pennie. "You have the face of a guilty Fair One. Tell us what crime you committed. And please, spare no detail."

"I just need a ride."

"I see." He turned back to chuckle with the other sipLips. "Transportation, then." He returned to Pennie. "Lucky for you we've had a cancellation today. I am Gavron." He extended his hand.

"Fair One PENN 1. Pennie," she said, shaking it quickly and then stepping back. Gavron's hand was caked in dirt and his nails were long and gray.

"I was told there'd be gifts?"

Pennie froze. "Gifts?"

"It's always nice to thank those who volunteer their time." He gestured back toward the smaller sipLips who had wandered off to kick at the garbage. "For the boys. Don't you think?"

Pennie pointed to the top of the pile.

Gavron spotted the container and released a few dribbles of spit, which slid down his chin. "Aim a little higher, boys," he said before whipping his dirty red hair out of his eyes and leaning into Pennie. "Couldn't smell their way into a garlic factory. Now. Where are we transporting you, exactly?"

"Down there," she whispered.

"Down *where*?" he whispered back.

"Earth."

Gavron threw his head back and laughed. "The *great* Fair Ones. Coddled with every kind of technological tool and yet they can't find a way down to Earth on their own. Ironic, no?" He leaned into Pennie again. "It's a nasty place. Why would you want to go there?"

She looked away.

"Why, Fair One?"

"I'm sorry, I don't think I should say."

"Then I don't think I should stay." Gavron snapped his fingers to get his boys' attention.

"Wait!" Pennie pleaded. "A Right to Delete. I have forty-eight hours."

"Ah. An RTD. Getting those horrid little clients to give up their elemental power. Rarely successful." He straightened up and flashed a smile. "However. It would be but a pleasure,

85

Fairly-est One. First, though, we eat. Right, boys? Climb!"

One of the sipLips rushed the pile of garbage, sliding back every few steps before gaining a little more ground. Once he reached the top, he snatched the container, surfed down the pile, and handed it to Gavron.

"Rocky Road froyo. How appropriate." Gavron produced a stroon from his robes and smiled at Pennie. "Cuz it's sure gonna be *that*." He glanced back to the other sipLips, who melted into fits of laughter, then lifted his stroon and dug in. "A few more minutes and we wouldn't have agreed to take you anywhere," he said with rocky road dribbling down his chin. "We don't like froyo milkshakes, do we, boys?"

The sipLips hovered behind him with smaller stroons, ready to pounce. "It's go time, boys." The sipLips rushed forward and devoured the Rocky Road. Finished within seconds, their chins were still dripping when Gavron threw the empty container over his head and onto the pile of garbage. He used his robes like a napkin, licked his stroon clean, and slipped it back into his pocket. The other sipLips did the same.

"Now then." He cleared his throat. "I'm sure you'll understand that travelling to the big E holds many risks. Risks that could—but *won't,* I assure you—end in an explosion." Gavron slugged a fist into his palm. "*Pow!*"

Pennie smiled weakly.

Gavron glanced down around her waist. "But just in case, in the *teensy weensy* chance of a sudden explosion, we'll need to ask you for a little, ooh, something for our time."

"I brought you the frozen yogurt," Pennie reminded him.

The sipLips chuckled and drooled.

"And it was *de*licious." Gavron slurped. "However, we were thinking of a more permanent gift. You know, like a few of your fancy Fair One gadgets."

The sipLips hooted.

Pennie threw open her hands. "I don't have any tools at all."

"How about stroons?"

"Sorry."

"And we're off, boys," Gavron snapped, spinning around and forming a huddle.

"No please!" Pennie rushed forward.

Gavron looked back at her pointedly. "We have a wave light surfing contest we forgot about. Encounter you later, Fairly One."

Their flimsy propellers began to turn in unison.

"You don't understand. I *have* to get down there. Fair Force has started the time," she held out her wrist.

Gavron eyed the stopwatch. "On second thought, what's the rush, boys?" The propellers came to a halt.

Pennie looked down at the stopwatch and then up at Gavron.

She shook her head. "I need this."

"Now here's where you're wrong, Fairest of the One. You won't be needing *any* of your tools on the big E. That's even against the rules for the rule-breakers."

"This was assigned to me *for* the trip."

Gavron stepped closer, ogling the watch. "Hel-*lo* beautiful purple creature." He smiled at the dinosaur. "Where've you been all my life?"

Pennie pulled her hand back and tucked it inside her robe. "I'll give you something from my tool belt when I return."

"Yeah. Nope." Gavron shook his head, a little dust flying off as he did.

She lowered her voice and tapped on her pocket. "I have an earpiece?"

He pulled a dozen tangled earpieces out of his robes. "Like these?"

Pennie flinched.

"You think you're the only desperate Fair One, Fair One?"

Pennie checked the stopwatch. **45:50:04**. More than two hours were gone. Tink said it was only a simple stopwatch, but what if it wasn't? What if the Fair Force couldn't locate her without it? Ever?

"Time's a tickin'," Gavron slurped.

She started to undo the watch. It was her only chance to save Tenley. It was the only chance to save herself. "Stop!"

From the top of the garbage pile, with his red beard blowing over his shoulder, Laraby looked down on them.

"Don't give that sipLip *anything*." He pointed at Gavron. "She brought you froyo."

Gavron opened his arms and chuckled. "It's a risky business, bro."

"It's nothing, Laraby. It's just a stopwatch," Pennie argued.

"Nothing? Every time these *things* get a piece of our equipment, they get closer to their goal." Laraby held his gaze on Gavron.

The smaller sipLips chuckled repulsively.

"What goal?" Pennie asked.

"Oh, you know," Gavron flapped his hand, "to take over the whole universe and all that. This side of it, anyway. That side's a little too outback for us."

"These sipLips are capable of things you can't even imagine, Pennie. Particularly this one. Isn't that right, Gavron?"

"Always bragging about me, aren't you, bro?" He beamed.

Pennie looked from Gavron to Laraby and back to Gavron.

"That's right. We're bros. As in *brothers*."

"Get out of here, Gavron." Laraby slid down the pile of garbage. "And take your mini-me's with you."

"Hey! Don't insult my boys. Don't *ever* insult my boys. It hurts their feelings." Gavron snapped the sipLips to attention. "Deal's off."

"Laraby," Pennie pleaded. "Do you have any other way of getting me down there?"

He hesitated, but shook his head.

"Well, I'm sorry then. I have no choice." Pennie handed Gavron the stopwatch, who deposited it into his robes faster than Laraby could react.

"What if it tracks you? How do you expect Fair Force to find you when the time's up?" Laraby asked.

Pennie's knees went weak.

"Give me a jingle. I'll come get you," Gavron said. He waved to his boys. "We're on again."

"I'm sorry, Laraby," Pennie mumbled.

"See you, L-train." Gavron yanked Pennie into their huddle. She gagged and coughed under their foul smell.

"Pennie! Don't leave!" Laraby shouted.

Their huddle began to shake.

Dirt started to fly.

And Pennie started to lift.

She could hear Laraby's voice wafting up to her.

The sipLips let out a sickening laugh. Everything swirled faster. Pennie felt her stomach jump into her mouth. Any moment now, her head would explode. Below her, she could just make out Laraby watching.

"Relax," Gavron shouted. "It's all downhill from here. After a little *up,* that is."

Pennie shuddered against a loud boom. Her tiny feet felt like they were being ripped from her body.

And then Gavron's laugh started to echo and everything went black.

17

45:37:17
Hadley Beach

Mrs. Tylwyth stopped the car.

"Thanks, Mom," Tenley said, opening her door and blowing a quick breath at the sky before jumping out. The rain directly above her stopped, but across the rest of the school parking lot the rain was falling hard.

"Okay, honey. Good luck."

Tenley clapped her paper pom-poms and shut the door. She looked up at the sky, blew out another quick breath above the path leading into school, and walked inside.

The auditorium stage was set with two podiums on either side of a larger podium. Dan Ringer was talking to a teacher below it.

"Hey, Danny," Tenley said with a big smile. "Like my pom-poms?" She shook them at him.

Dan glanced at her. "Are you here for the auditions?"

"Y-E-S!" she cheered.

"Great. We're not quite finished setting up." He turned back to the teacher.

"Looks good, Dan," the teacher, whom Tenley vaguely recognized from her second period English class, told him. "I think we can get started."

"Very good, sir." Dan tried to spin away, but spun into Tenley instead. "Sorry."

"So where do you want me?" She flipped her hair.

"Everyone is back there, through that door." Dan waved to the right.

"Super!" Tenley skipped away.

Backstage, girls and boys were pacing and mumbling to themselves.

"Excuse me." Tenley tapped a small brunette with earbuds sprouting out both ears.

The brunette ignored her.

"Hey!" Tenley said, this time forcing her way into the brunette's line of vision and snapping.

The brunette popped one earbud out.

"Hi. Thanks. I couldn't help noticing your awesome nail beds."

"What?"

Pennie pointed to the girl's fingers.

"I just wanted to ask if you'd been watching my nail art tutorials on YouTube?"

The girl crinkled her nose and looked at her fingers. "No."

"I post them daily. Tenley Tylwyth's Nail Art Tutorials. I'm running for America's Next Most Inspirational Teen. Building confidence one nail at a time." Tenley smiled. "Sure would appreciate your vote."

The brunette popped her earbud back in and looked over Tenley's shoulder.

Through the curtain wings, they could see Dan Ringer stepping onto the stage. The contestants started lining up in pairs.

"Excuse me," Tenley asked them. "Would anyone mind if I went first?"

The confused boy at the front of the line was the only one to respond. "What?"

"Thanks. Auditions are kind of my thing," Tenley straightened her sash and slipped into his spot.

"Ladies and gentleman, thank you for coming today and cheering these middle-school students on," Dan greeted the crowd. "There are pamphlets at the back explaining how to get more involved. Remember, there are hundreds of kids who struggle with literacy every day. Reading shouldn't be a privilege. And spelling should be fun!"

"He's even hotter and more inspirational behind a microphone," Tenley mumbled. She turned back to the boy. "He's not trying out for ANMIT, is he?"

The boy shrugged.

"Let's have the first two contestants come on out. Roberta Robb and Jorge Menendez!" Dan Ringer announced.

Tenley thrust herself forward, leaving a confused Jorge Menendez behind.

93

Rather than go to one of the podiums, Tenley took to center stage and clapped her pom-poms. "Hey everyone. Let's hear it for *Hadley Beach! Hadley Beach! Go, Hadley Beach!*" She added a high kick.

The students, upon noticing Tenley's homemade tutu and pom-poms, started laughing.

Tenley shook the pom-poms harder. "C-O-M-P-E-T-I-T-I-O-N! What does it spell?" she asked the crowd.

"*Nice outfit!*" they yelled back.

Dan lifted his hand to quiet them. "All right. We need to get going. There are a lot of you here tonight and only a few spots to move on to the regional level. Remember, those of you who are eliminated need to exit immediately so we can keep the competition moving. Let's begin!" He walked over to Tenley. "What happened to Jorge?"

"He let me go F-I-R-S-T!" Tenley bopped him once on the shoulder with her pom-pom.

"And your name is?"

Tenley looked stunned. "Tenley Tylwyth." She bopped him harder this time.

Dan scribbled it down and returned to center stage. "Well, it's cool to see such enthusiasm for tryouts this year. Let's hear it for word nerds!"

The gym erupted.

Dan Ringer raised both hands to quiet the crowd. "Okay. So, Tenley, we'll start with you."

"Great. And I just want to say that I would be so honored to represent Hadley Middle School on America's Next Most

Inspirational Teen, which is holding nominations Friday. I promise each and every one of you that my nails and I will look our personal best."

A few loners in the crowd clapped lamely.

"Hey!" someone yelled out. "Last year's winner on that show gave Beats headphones to their entire school."

"Y.E.S!" Tenley clapped her pom-poms.

Dan Ringer cleared his throat. "Here we go." He picked up an index card. "'Triumphant'."

Tenley went blank.

"The word is 'triumphant'," Dan repeated.

Tenley looked at the audience, at the judges, and then at Roberta Robb, all of whom were staring back at her.

"Tenley. You have ten seconds."

The audience shuffled.

Tenley broke out into a mega-watt smile and walked around the podium. "Give me a T, give me an R, give me an I, give me a—" She stopped with a blank look.

The tension in the auditorium was palpable.

For half a second, Tenley's expression fell, until she broke into another mega-watt smile.

"I'll tell you how to how to spell *triumphant*! H-A-D-L-E-Y-M-I-D-D-L-E-S-C-H-O-O-L!"

The audience clapped halfheartedly. Tenley curtsied, waved, curtsied again, and slipped behind her podium, still waving.

"I'm sorry, Tenley, that is incorrect. Thank you for coming today," Dan said, showing her the exit.

Tenley leaned into her microphone. "Don't forget. On

Sunday, text ANMIT: T.E.N.L.E.Y.T."

Someone threw a water bottle at her. Undaunted, Tenley reached into her sleeve, pulled out a handful of glitter and threw it at the audience before walking off the stage.

18

42:58:43
Hadley Beach

Something sharp was jabbing into her side. Pennie opened her eyes.

Branches.

Poking her.

Real branches.

The kind that could only be found on Earth.

Pennie jolted upright and hit the ground.

She moaned. She'd landed in a tree. The one she'd just fallen out of.

Her head felt like it was splitting down the middle. She reached for her tool belt before remembering she didn't have it. She lifted her wrist to look at her stopwatch, before remembering she didn't have that either.

"Gavron?" Pennie whispered. "Gavron?"

But Gavron was not there. And there weren't any slurps or drools coming from anywhere, either.

She tried to stand, but must have forgotten about the house on her back. Or maybe it was a small meteor. Something very heavy was preventing her from standing. She pushed against the ground with all her might and got to her knees.

Gravity, she remembered. That's what it was.

Using the $3^{rd}i$, it was impossible to believe that gravity could be so heavy. It was invisible, after all! *"Breathe,"* Laraby had told her.

Pennie tried to sip in the thick air, but her heart was racing. Everything was too bright. And pointy. And *heavy*. She sipped in more air until slowly, slowly, using the closest tree for support, she pulled herself up to standing.

Through the maze of branches, she saw it: a house. The Tylwyth house.

She was here, at 19 Nathan Lane. *On Earth*!

She gritted her teeth and took a baby step toward the yard. How could her tiny feet be this heavy? By the time she reached the end of the tree line, beads of sweat were slipping down her temples.

But the sky!

"So bright," she said, reaching up for it. No one had ever come close to describing the sheer beauty of it from this point of view.

She looked across the luscious green grass. "I can't believe I'm here," she whispered to the trees. Acclimating to Earth took a few days—she knew that part. But no one had told her about the birds chirping or the leaves blowing. Everywhere she looked, there was color and movement and energy. And all of it was spectacular.

A searing pain ripped through the back of her knee. She yelped and yanked up her robes to slap at the burn. A bee fell to the grass. She jumped away. "Why did you do that?"

But the bee didn't respond. And without her tools, a bee couldn't hear her.

Plus, she'd killed it. "Oh no. I didn't mean—I'm sorry," she whispered. It was said that Mother Nature kept tabs on each and every one of Earth's creatures. She didn't have control over the animal kingdom, but she held a grudge against anyone who'd harmed any animal in it.

Another buzz blew by. Pennie looked across the lawn.

Mrs. Tylwyth's car was gone. Along the side of the house, Tenley's old princess playhouse looked exactly like it had through the 3rd i: dirty and abandoned.

Pennie placed her hands under the back of her knee, lifted her boulder/leg, and slung it forward. She did the same with the other leg until she'd walked out of the woods. A squirrel crossed the yard and stopped to stare at her.

"Hey, you furry thing."

The squirrel cocked its head.

"I've just arrived here. My first time."

The squirrel scurried away.

"Rude," Pennie mumbled, struggling on. Tenley, as usual, had left the front door open. Which, today, was good news. Pennie stepped in and shut the door.

Everything was familiar. The 3^{rd}i, equipped with technology so advanced it had its own vocabulary, could see inside and under just about every spot on Earth. But standing *in* this place was so much different. The colors in the hallway looked rich enough to dip a finger into. And the smells. There was little to smell in Fair City besides rock and dust and Administrator contempt. In Tenley's house, the smells were full of things that made you feel *alive*.

Pennie peeked into the kitchen. Her eyes fell to the clock on the wall: 1:25 p.m. She was five hours and twenty-five minutes into her mission. There was plenty of time to convince Tenley to stop using her element. Now she just needed to find her.

She turned for the door and stopped. Her robes.

By the time Pennie made her way up the stairs (sitting on each step for a good thirty seconds before starting up again) and into Tenley's room, it was 1:40 p.m. The room was so pink she had to close her eyes and hold onto the wall to get her balance. The curtains, the walls, the bedspread, and even the chair were bright enough to feel the heat coming off them.

Pennie tripped over a (pink) high-top to get to the mirror. A kind of squeak fell out of her when she saw her reflection. She was a mess, worse than she'd imagined. Her long red hair had fallen halfway out of its tight bun, her usual ivory-white face was smudged with soot, dried tears had dripped out of her gray eyes and made a pathway down both cheeks, and her robes were so filthy she could have been mistaken for a sipLip.

In the bathroom (pink) she used a washcloth (pink) to clean up, and a brush (pink) to straighten down her red hair. Then she opened Tenley's closet and stared at shoes and jackets, scarves, jeans, and dresses. She'd seen these all before, but the idea of *wearing* them? Never.

A few minutes later, Pennie was dressed in the only clothes that fit her small frame: a pink miniskirt, pink leggings, and a pink T-shirt under a pink hoodie, plus the partner to the pink high-top she had tripped over—which was at least three sizes too big.

After she put the other shoe on—so squishy and soft, so much better than her simple flat slippers—she came up with the perfect place to hide her grimy robes: the princess playhouse. She gathered the robes together. Something fell out.

Tink's crystal eight.

Pennie slipped the necklace over her head and tucked the crystal under her T-shirt. The glowing crystal eight didn't look anything human-made. She'd have to keep it hidden. She hurried out the door and over to the stairs, amazed at how much easier it was going down.

19

41:55:14
Hadley Beach

Pennie turned left at the end of the driveway and tripped. The shoes were huge on her. She heard a car and scurried behind the closest tree until it passed. As soon as she stepped out again, another car went by, and then another. No one seemed to notice her.

After yet another car whizzed by she realized why: there was nothing *to* notice. She looked like any other teenager, just pinker and smaller, heading for school. She tucked her red hair behind her ear and started down the sidewalk again. And tripped. At least Hadley Middle School was close.

***

"What is *that*?" a girl asked, looking out the classroom window.

Three heads turned to look.

"What is she wearing?"

"Seriously."

"What's with that hair?"

Outside, Pennie stopped to catch her breath.

"Those are ginger extensions, totally."

"Gingers can't grow their hair that long."

"I know, right?"

Tenley, out of her paper tutu and back in her regular clothes, sitting a row back from these girls, leaned forward. "Who are you talking about?"

"Her." One of the girls pointed out the window.

Tenley smiled. "I've never seen her before. Who is she?"

The girls shrugged.

"I bet she's here to see me. I bet she's come to see the Ginger Ninja!"

The girls sneered at Tenley.

Mr. Peddle pointed his chalk at them. "Quiet down, girls," he warned from the blackboard.

As soon as he turned back to the board, the girls pulled out their phones and started texting each other.

"Is she for realsies?" one of the girls whispered, glancing back at Tenley.

"A ginger ninja. What does that even mean?"

"She's such a loser," another one of the girls whispered loud enough for Tenley to hear.

Tenley looked down at her schoolwork and pretended to

take notes.

"Omigod. It's *her*," one of the girls said, texting it at the same time.

Everyone in the room looked over at the door.

"Can I help you?" Mr. Peddle asked.

Pennie could only pant.

"Freak," someone mumbled.

"Maybe she's escaped from a pink ginger prison or something," one of the girls whispered.

"Are you looking for the principal's office, young lady?" Mr. Peddle asked, putting down his chalk.

Tenley stood. "Mr. Puddle, I think the ginger is looking for me, Tenley T., Ginger Ninja."

Pennie beamed. *Tenley*. Her client. Standing right there!

"*Peddle*. I'm going to have to call the office." Mr. Peddle picked up the classroom phone.

Tenley waved Pennie over. Pennie shuffled her way through the classroom, panting and sweating, pushing off desk arms and unsuspecting shoulders, while the students mocked her behind her back.

When Pennie reached Tenley, she threw her arms around her.

Tenley Tylwyth. Her Tenley Tylwyth.

Tenley peeled Pennie off. "It's overwhelming to find someone who will finally speak for you, ginger. I can see that. But maybe, can you take a step back. Or two?"

Pennie stroked Tenley's blond hair. The class broke out in fits of laughter.

"All right, you two," Mr. Peddle said. "What's going on back there?"

"Sorry, Mr. Piddle," Tenley said.

"*Peddle*, Miss Tylwyth. And who are you, Miss—"

"Pennie. My name is Pennie, um, *one*."

"Okay, Miss One." Mr. Peddle pointed his chalk at her. "I'm going to have to ask you to go to the office and get a visitor's pass. End of the hallway, first right."

Not wanting to make more of a scene, Pennie gave Tenley a last look and panted her way slowly toward the door.

Mr. Peddle turned back to the board. "The rest of class, we'll get back to the War of 1812. Can anyone tell me when this war took place?"

One of the girls twisted around to Tenley. "Hey, Tylwyth, why didn't you tell us you had a ginger sister?"

"I don't," Tenley said, watching Pennie struggle along with everyone else.

"Cousin?" one of the other girls asked.

"No," Tenley shook her head.

"So why is she wearing your shoes? You wrote on them, remember?"

They all looked at Pennie's shoes before she stepped out of the room. *Vote for Me, Tenley T!* was written along the sides of both soles. Tenley's mouth dropped open.

20

41:50:53
Hadley Beach

"What did you do with my mother after you broke into our house and stole my clothes?"

"She wasn't even home."

"So you *were* in our house." Tenley slapped her hand over her mouth.

"Yes, except I promise. I'm not here to hurt you or your mother. I'd never hurt your mother. She's the sweetest woman on the planet, from what I can see."

Tenley glared at Pennie "You've been watching my mother?"

"Only when she's with you."

"I'm going to call the police." Tenley started through the crowded hallway to her locker.

Pennie pushed herself off the wall where she'd stayed hidden, waiting for the bell to ring. "Wait," she said, following as fast as she could.

At her locker, Tenley pulled out her cell phone.

"Please just listen to me," Pennie panted. "I've come to help you."

Tenley lowered her phone. "With the auditions?"

"No, not exactly. I need you to sign a form." Pennie caught her breath. "A short hologram form."

"What *form*? Are you trying to get me *not* to do the auditions? Listen, person. There can only be *one* Hadley Beach nominee for America's Next Most Inspirational Teen. And that nominee stands for gingers and does nail art tutorials. Not wearing weird amounts of pink and panting."

"I'm not trying to get nominated for anything, Tenley." A hurried boy bumped into her, throwing Pennie off balance. He mumbled a "sorry" and kept going.

Tenley considered her. "Do you have a ginger problem I can help you with?"

"No. It's nothing like that either."

"So you're just a stalker?" Tenley lifted her phone again.

"I'm not a stalker."

The next bell rang.

"I have class. Why don't you go back to whatever hospital you ran away from? Leave my mother and me alone."

Tenley started down a different hallway. It was getting harder for Pennie to keep up. Every time she stopped, gravity caught up with her, making it even more difficult to get going again.

"Tenley, please."

Tenley frowned back at her. "What's the matter with you? I know gingers can't run as fast as normal people, but I mean, seriously?"

"I'm a little jet-lagged."

Tenley spotted Dan Ringer coming toward her.

"Hey Danny," she slowed. "What are you doing here?"

Dan ignored her and stared at Pennie instead. He stared so hard, in fact, he walked straight into a girl carrying a stack of books.

"I'm sorry," Dan apologized, collecting the books. He handed the girl her pile and disappeared into a wave of students.

"Do you *know* who that was?" Tenley asked Pennie.

"No."

"Dan *Ringer*. He's in high school. He's so hot." Tenley started down the hall again.

"Hey! You two! Just where do you think you're going?"

It was a PE-looking teacher, tall enough to hover over both of them.

Tenley straightened her sash. "To PE. I don't want to be late. There's a mean sub today." She walked away quickly.

"Me neither," Pennie said, feebly shuffling after Tenley. There was no chance of catching her, though. Exhausted, Pennie watched Tenley slip through a doorway.

Pennie stumbled. Her vision began to blur. She needed to sleep. Just a little nap, she thought, slumping back against the wall. Something pinched her ear.

"Ow."

"You must be the one waiting for new PE clothes. I don't

understand how you girls can lose your clothes so often." The teacher yanked Pennie by the ear and pulled her over to a closet door. "Used to be, kids, they kept their clothes for the entire school year."

She unlocked the door with a jumbled set of keys and flipped on the light. "Go on in and get your size. Speedy quick."

Pennie blinked at her.

"Can. You. Hear. Me?" the teacher asked with a sudden flash of concern.

Pennie nodded.

"Then you got a problem with me or something? I might be a sub, but this coach doesn't take any you-know-what from any kids. And I know exactly where the principal's office is. I even know where the *assistant* principal's office is. So get your clothes. Now."

Motionless for too long again, Pennie clenched her teeth and fought her way through gravity and into the closet. She grabbed a pair of extra-small shorts and a shirt, and shuffled her way out. "Not much of a sprinter, I see," the teacher clucked before pulling the door shut and starting down the hall. Pennie grabbed onto the wall.

"Did you hear me?" The teacher turned around at the girl's locker room. "I said you've got three minutes to get changed and be on the court." She pulled open the door. "Maybe I'm not Coach Stevens. But I *am* Coach Lesnit."

Inside the locker room, a few of Tenley's classmates were climbing into their PE clothes. Pennie smiled. They whispered. Through the gym doorway, Pennie spotted Tenley. Her sash was cinched across her PE shirt.

Pennie found a corner to slip the clothes on and a few minutes later, swimming in the T-shirt and shorts, she walked out into the gym. Coach Lesnit's back was turned to her. Tenley and the rest of the girls were scrimmaging on the court. Pennie dragged herself up to the top of the bleachers.

"Pass it to me, Makayla." Tenley flagged her teammate. "Look. I'm open!"

Makayla did look, but handed the basketball off to another player instead, who had it quickly stolen by her opponent, who scored.

Tenley glared at Makayla. "I told you, I was *open*! I need an action shot." She pointed to a girl on the bleachers holding up her phone, ready to take a photo.

Makayla brushed her off. "You're not even going to get that stupid nomination."

Tenley's face darkened.

Pennie recognized that look. "Oh no," she said, reaching down for her tool belt, which wasn't there. "Tenley, don't—"

But Makayla was already on the ground.

"*Tenley,*" Pennie grumbled. No one else, not even Makayla herself, could have suspected Tenley had knocked her down. The rogue gust of wind disappeared just as silently as it had come.

"Time out." Coach Lesnit blew her whistle and waved the squad over to the bleachers, where she pulled out a big cardboard box.

No one noticed Pennie on the bleachers above them.

"I'm not much of a bragger, but you're looking at a National

110

Fencing Champ." Coach Lesnit poked her thumb into her chest. "What that means is, you're dealing with an expert. Fencing doesn't just require skill, it requires *patience*. Something your generation is lacking entirely. So today, we're going to try it. Who's excited?"

The girls scoffed. "That's like *ancient*," one of them said.

Coach Lesnit scanned the room. "Volunteers? You." She pointed to a skinny girl. "You look like you could be an athlete if you ate a steak every once in a while."

The skinny girl walked to Coach Lesnit, who began fitting her with gear, leaving ample opportunity for the girls to pull their phones out of their bras and start texting.

Pennie scooted down the bleachers and slid in beside Tenley.

"Are you *kidding* me?" Tenley slid away.

"Hey, quiet over there." Coach Lesnit glared. "Girls in the first row, come over and help me." She turned back to the skinny girl, who looked terrified now.

"I saw what you just did out there," Pennie whispered.

Tenley frowned. "Yeah. I *didn't* get a shot of me scoring."

"No. What you did with wind."

Tenley flinched. "I don't know what you're talking about."

"Yes, you do. You know exactly what I'm talking about. And you've got to stop."

"You're crazy."

"You're in danger."

Tenley crossed her arms. "Why don't you go spread your weirdness on someone else."

"You still suck your middle finger at night."

111

Tenley's cheeks fell.

"You do," Pennie said.

Tenley looked down at her phone. "If you leave now, I won't turn you in to the principal."

"And you know what else you do? You write a note to your father asking him to come back from Alaska."

"Wow," Tenley said after a pause. "That must have been *really* hard getting into the school files and reading up about me." She flicked her eyebrows at the pink leggings Pennie had kept on under her gym shorts. "And anyway, I know you're trying to freak me out so *you* can be nominated for ANMIT. You probably even transferred here because you didn't get the vote in your last school district."

Pennie exhaled. This was going to be harder than she thought.

"You never send them to him, though, the letters."

This time, Tenley's cheeks flamed. She looked up from her phone. "I've lost two followers. Do you know what a follower is?" she asked Pennie. "A *vote*. A follower is a vote. I need to be out there, mingling. Not sitting here with you." She narrowed her eyes at Pennie and pursed her lips. Her face darkened.

"No!" Pennie warned her. "Don't do it. If I go flying through the air, everyone will see."

Tenley looked down at the court. Pennie was right; a few girls were staring up at them.

Pennie lowered her voice. "You have to stop using your wind element."

Tenley looked away.

"Tenley? Did you hear me? You can't just blow things away when you feel like it."

"Fine!" she said.

"Really?" Pennie asked, surprised.

Tenley didn't respond.

"Okay. That's great." Pennie leaned back, relieved. "We can sign the form at your house." She yawned. "Now if you don't mind, I'm going to close my eyes and take a little nap."

"*Stalker!*"

"Who just yelled?" Coach Lesnit spun around with her hands on her hips.

"*She* did!" Tenley pointed at Pennie.

The coach scowled at her. "I knew you were going to be trouble. It's always the wimpy ones." She pointed to the door. "Principal's office. Now."

Pennie shook her head at Tenley. "You're running out of time," she whispered, stepping off the bleachers and shuffling toward the exit.

Alone in the locker room, Pennie struggled out of the PE clothes. She dozed off for a few seconds before lacing up the second pink sneaker. The air was excruciatingly heavy now.

She stepped out of the locker room and into the hallway, where Dan Ringer was standing with a teacher.

Her vision began swirling again.

This trip to Earth was nothing but a dream. A very heavy dream.

A smile crossed Pennie's lips just as she felt a knock on her head.

21

"Tenley? Come open the door for me, please."

Pennie blinked her eyes open. This was not her flat in Fair City. She reached down for her tool belt. Where were her robes? Why was she wearing all pink?

"Tenley?" Mrs. Tylwyth repeated from the behind the front door.

"I'm doing my nails, Mom," Tenley called down the stairs.

The Tylwyth couch. The Tylwyth living room. On Earth. That's where she was. Pennie sat up.

The last thing she remembered was walking toward the school exit and that knock on her head.

She got herself up on shaky legs and peeked around the corner. Through the kitchen window, she saw Mrs. Tylwyth lifting groceries out of her trunk.

114

Mrs. Tylwyth!

Pennie watched her struggle with her bags. One of them dropped onto the driveway. She needed help. Pennie shuffled over and opened the front door.

"Oh!" Mrs. Tylwyth took a step back. "Well, hello there," she smiled. "Are you feeling better?"

"Yes, thank you." Pennie looked down at the groceries. "Can I help you with those?"

"Oh gracious, no. Don't be silly. You're the one who fainted. Please go back in and sit down. I went to get some groceries, you look like you haven't eaten in, well ... I hope I'm not sounding too forward. How long have you been a classmate of Tenley's exactly?" Mrs. Tylwyth was trying to sound casual, but her brow betrayed her. She stole a look at Tenley's high-tops as she walked past Pennie and into the kitchen.

"I don't go to Hadley Middle School, Mrs. Tylwyth."

When Mrs. Tylwyth turned around, she had a quizzical look on her face.

"What did you say your name was?"

"Pennie."

"And your last name?'

"Just—" she mumbled. "One?"

"I knew it!" Mrs. Tylwyth rushed up to her. "You wouldn't happen to know Gertrude Justwan, would you?" She winked.

"Gerty?" Pennie asked. Of course she did. Gerty was Tenley's nanny. She had taken care of Tenley whenever Mrs. Tylwyth was working at the antique store.

"This is so wonderful!" Mrs. Tylwyth pulled Pennie into a

bear hug. "I couldn't tell when I first saw you, because of course you were lying down asleep in the nurse's office by the time I got there. I came as soon as Mr. Frimpy called me. Then that nice high school boy helped us get you into the car so I could bring you back here and put you on the couch. Do you remember walking into the house? You were still terribly exhausted, I'm afraid. But anywho. You have the same ears!" She tugged at them.

"I do?"

"Yes! Now don't tell me you've never been told you look like Gerty before. Spitting image. Let's go tell Tenley; she'll be tickled."

"I'm not sure Tenley wants to see me."

"You came all the way here," Mrs. Tylwyth protested. "Of course she wants to see you. Now that we know who you are. Gerty's daughter!" She grabbed Pennie's hand and dragged her up the stairs.

Mrs. Tylwyth knocked softly on Tenley's door. "Tenley, I've got some exciting news!"

Pennie braced herself.

"Pennie is Gerty's daughter!"

Tenley's door swung open. "Gerty's daughter?"

Mrs. Tylwyth turned to Pennie. "Has Gerty moved back to California then?"

Pennie had to think about this. The last time she saw Gerty was when she was here, taking care of Tenley in this house. "No I haven't seen her in ... well ... she's gone." Pennie looked down solemnly.

Mrs. Tylwyth slapped her hand over her mouth. "You don't mean?" She pulled Pennie in tightly. "You poor thing. The last time I heard from her she was opening a gift shop in the Keys. I'm embarrassed to say I thought she said her daughter's name was Annabel, but there's no mistaking this hair. Exactly the same as Gerty's. Right ,Tenley?"

Tenley narrowed her eyes at Pennie. "So you're really not trying to get nominated for ANMIT?"

"No," Pennie mumbled into Mrs. Tylwyth's chest.

"You can stay with us for as long as you'd like." Mrs. Tylwyth released her. "Tomorrow, I'll register you at the middle school."

"I'm only here for a short stay."

"And you can sleep right here with Tenley," Mrs. Tylwyth ignored her. "I would do anything for your mother. She was a wonderful woman." Her eyes filled with tears. "She took such good care of my Tenley. And now I get to return the favor."

"Mrs. Tylwyth, I really appreciate it, thank you. I'm just staying for a day or two though."

Mrs. Tylwyth was hearing none of it. "We'll have to write Mr. Tylwyth and tell him the happy news." She winked at Tenley, then squeezed Pennie's hand and walked out the door.

Tenley groaned. "She means it when she says she's gonna write him. As in by *snail mail*. They don't have Internet on fishing rigs. It takes like *two months* to get a letter from him."

Pennie tried to look surprised.

Tenley walked over to her desk. "I hardly even *remember* your mother. She only took care of me until I was, like, ten."

"She was nice, Tenley." Pennie walked into the room.

117

"Yeah. Sorry." Tenley grabbed her phone and started texting. "As long as you'll be staying here now, will you be in my nail art tutorial?"

Pennie looked down at her hands. "Okay."

"Good." Tenley smiled without looking up.

Pennie noticed the digital clock next to the bed. It was already five o'clock. Time went so fast on Earth. "*If* you'll agree to do what we talked about at school. Sign the form I need you to sign." Pennie brought her hand to her temple. She was about to produce the hologram contract when Mrs. Tylwyth peeked into the room again.

"Girls? How about a shopping spree? I think Pennie's going to need some new clothes."

"Shopping spree! Let's go!"

Tenley pushed by Pennie and ran out the door.

22

38:10:33
Hadley Beach

The mall was packed.

"This is perfect. I needed nomination clothes anyway." Tenley hurried ahead.

It was taxing, trying to keep up with her. Already, Pennie was out of breath and they'd only just stepped into the mall.

Mrs. Tylwyth looked concerned for Pennie. "Tenley, could you slow down a bit?"

Tenley was a few stores ahead and showed no signs of slowing. A posse of girls about the same age as Tenley sneered at her as she hurried by.

"What's with the sash?" One of them, a brunette with blond tips at the end of her long hair, scowled.

"Is she like a beauty contestant or something?"

"Toddlers and tiaras."

"*Right?*" another girl snorted.

Pennie glared at them.

Mrs. Tylwyth looked worried when Pennie wiped her brow. An old lady with an oxygen tank sped by them.

"Let's take a little rest, shall we?" Mrs. Tylwyth suggested.

Up ahead, Tenley disappeared into a store. "Thanks, Mrs. Tylwyth. Maybe just until I catch my breath."

"You must be tired from the long trip. Florida is across the country."

"It was a long trip," Pennie agreed.

Mrs. Tylwyth led Pennie over to an empty table at the edge of the food court. Pennie dropped into a chair.

"Now that does feel nice," Mrs. Tylwyth sighed into her seat. A father and toddler walked by holding hands.

"Did Gerty ever tell you that Tenley's father's has had a terrible time getting off work to come visit?"

For the past twelve years? Pennie wanted to say, but instead she nodded. Even Gerty used to fall for the letters Mrs. Tylwyth wrote, painstakingly concealing her own penmanship so Tenley would believe they were from her father. "Yes, I remember her saying something about that," Pennie said. "That's too bad."

Mrs. Tylwyth looked out at the crowd of mall-goers.

A small girl ran after her older sister and tripped. The mother swept the wailing girl up and held a tissue to her lip. "I told you not to chase your sister like that."

The little girl nodded through her tears and hugged her mom.

Mrs. Tylwyth smiled at the scene. "Funny, I don't remember Tenley ever having little accidents like that. I used to joke with her that she was born with bubble wrap around her. She just never seemed to get hurt."

Pennie shuffled in her seat. "I remember."

"You do?" Mrs. Tylwyth turned to her, frowning.

"I mean, yeah. Because Gerty told me that, too. She told me everything about you guys."

Mrs. Tylwyth beamed. "Actually it doesn't surprise me that Gerty told you all about Tenley. Those two were very close."

"Gerty sure did love her."

"Did she tell you about the time that Tenley nearly fell off her bike and broke her arm?"

"But she didn't break her arm. *Or* fall off her bike," Pennie remembered.

"It was close though," Mrs. Tylwyth agreed. "To this day, we still don't know how that bike managed to keep itself upright like that. It was like the wind caught her, which sounds crazy, I know."

"Crazy," Pennie mumbled.

"And then there was the time that a horse came *this close* to running her over."

"Horse?"

"Let me think now, it was at some kind of event."

"The pony rides!" Pennie said, immediately regretting it. Was Mrs. Tylwyth going to believe Gerty told her *all* of this?

Luckily, Mrs. Tylwyth appeared to be lost in her memories. "Pony rides, that's right. One got loose and ran straight for her. She was only about four years old. It stopped a few inches in front of her and then just, *zip*, practically flew backwards. That *was* strange."

"Yeah. Really strange."

"There was the time in Super Toys, too. As soon as we got there, torrential rain came out of nowhere. It was like a mini hurricane right over the store. Later we learned it had only sprinkled everywhere else. Anyway, while we were waiting for the storm to pass I couldn't find Tenley. The manager called the police and they finally found her tucked away behind a shelf of Barbies, taking every one out of their boxes. She had gone through almost all the boxes by the time we found her. Did Gerty tell you about that?"

Pennie nodded. A sticky feeling started in her stomach. How could she have let Tenley be so reckless with her element? Turning a slight rainfall into a hurricane over the store so she could play with all those Barbies. It seemed so innocent at the time.

"It's as if Tenley has always had some sort of Fairy Godmother watching out for her." Mrs. Tylwyth giggled. "Silly thought, I know."

"Very silly," Pennie said quietly. The Fairships were right. Tenley could have been discovered by Mother Nature dozens of times by now. Pennie had only ever wanted to see her client happy and using her element always managed to do that. Growing up without a father was hard; the least Pennie could do was let her have a bit of fun with her power. But she'd gone too far.

"Pennie, dear. Did you hear me?" Mrs. Tylwyth was staring at her. "I was saying that Gerty did a good job raising you."

"Mom!" Tenley waved from a kiosk in the middle of the mall. *Tranquility Stones for your Water Fixtures* was on the sign.

Shiny stones were piled up high.

"Coming!" Mrs. Tylwyth got to her feet. "Ready, Pennie dear?"

Pennie struggled to stand. When she got back to Fair City, she was going to have to start working out at the Asteroid gym.

"Mom, wouldn't this look great in my nail tutorial?" Tenley held out a smooth oval rock with *WISDOM* etched into it. "I could hold my hand over it like this?" She petted the rock. "Or I could use this?" She picked up another rock. This one read, *THINK.*

"*Think?*" Mrs. Tylwyth chuckled. "What's tranquil about that?"

The brunette with the blond tips walked around from the neighboring kiosk. Her posse of girls appeared behind her with the same snarky grins on their faces. "Almost too good. Am I right? An ugly mom and a loser sister for the beauty queen wannabe."

Tenley's face drained. She turned to the girl, gripping the *Think* rock so hard her knuckles were white. "What did you just say about my mom?"

Pennie reached out for Tenley's shoulder. "Put the rock down."

Tenley pulled away, keeping her eyes trained on the girl who stood taller and crossed her arms. "What's your talent gonna be, wannabe? Texting?"

Tenley blinked at the girl, considering.

"Tenley, give me the rock," Pennie said.

"How about we come back another time, honey?" Mrs. Tylwyth suggested.

"Did you hear what she just called you, Mom?"

"I didn't hear a thing. Let's go." Mrs. Tylwyth started for the exit.

"Better follow Mommy," the girl snickered.

Pennie stepped closer to Tenley. "She's not worth it. Don't risk your chances of getting nominated. Everyone in here has a cell phone. You don't want to see yourself on the Internet like this."

After a beat, Tenley looked down at the rock. "You're right. I'm not losing ANMIT over that mutant."

She placed the rock back down on top of the pile and started after her mother.

Pennie watched the posse of girls high-five their leader before she turned away in the pink high-tops and followed Tenley.

Just as they reached the exit, the girl shouted, "See ya, losers. And your mom *is* ugly!"

That was it. Tenley spun around, pursed her lips, and blew out a fast hard breath before Pennie could stop her.

The *Think* rock lifted into the air and idled for a split second before hurling toward the girl, narrowly missing her head and shattering a glass window behind her.

Mayhem ensued. Alarms went off and security guards rushed out of doorways.

"Oh my word." Mrs. Tylwyth put her hand on her cheek. "What happened?"

Pennie fumed.

"Dunno." Tenley shrugged, steering a confused Mrs. Tylwyth out the door.

23

36:30:15
Hadley Beach

Later, after Mrs. Tylwyth's delicious dinner of macaroni and cheese and salami sandwiches, the best things Pennie had ever tasted, Pennie agreed to help Tenley with her nail tutorial.

"Thanks for dinner, Mom. I'm doing tribal art nails tonight."

"That sounds exotic," Mrs. Tylwyth said, starting on the dishes.

"Come on, Pennie, let's go." Tenley cleared her plate and hurried out of the kitchen.

"That was the best meal I've ever had, Mrs. Tylwyth. Thank you," Pennie said, clearing her plate as well.

"Oh, don't be silly. Tomorrow I'll make something a little more interesting. Go on up and help Tenley. I know she appreciates it."

Pennie gave Mrs. Tylwyth a smile. Alone with Tenley, she'd

finally get her to sign the form. "Thanks again, Mrs. Tylwyth."

Pennie crawled her way up the stairs. With a full belly now, fatigue was washing over her like high tide.

Tenley was standing by the cardboard backdrop she'd made for her nail tutorials. She directed an exhausted-looking Pennie to sit in the beanbag and frowned at her. "You probably need to get in better shape before the next PE class. You're not going to pass run day. Mrs. Arrowbad is evil. You could have a broken leg, and she'd still make you run."

"We need to talk," Pennie said.

"Not now. I'm about to start recording." She nodded to the shoe box she'd taken the top off of. Inside was a miniature living room set. A tiny yellow rug lined the bottom and a miniature plastic chair was placed in the corner. "This is called 'the fingernail set.' I made it myself. Okay, so basically, I do all the talking and designing and you just place your hand on the rug and watch. I'm the only one on camera. Let me see your nails."

Pennie held out her hands. "We're not doing the feet, right?" She didn't want Tenley to see how little they were.

Tenley pulled a face at Pennie's fingernails. "Those are even shorter than my mom's."

"They like us to keep them this way." Some of their tools required very precise manual implementation.

"Who's *they*?"

"Did I say 'they'? I meant at my old school, I used to do a lot of finger things." She cleared her throat. "So tribal art, what is that exactly, anyway?"

"No offense, but your nails are way too short. I'm going to

have to give you acrylic tips, okay?"

"I need to talk to you first, though."

Before she could tap her temple, Tenley grabbed Pennie's hands.

"It'll just take like ten minutes. Hold your hands right here."

It was true; Tenley was a master with nails. Pennie watched her short plain fingers transform into long elegant digits.

"Told you," Tenley said. "Do you have to go to the bathroom or anything? ' Cause once I start videoing I don't like to stop."

Pennie shook her head.

"Great. Shh!"

Tenley started her commentating.

Much later, Pennie had an elaborate tribal design on each nail.

Tenley stopped the recording on her cell phone. Pennie had stayed quiet during the entire tutorial, wherein Tenley had been all business, keeping her comments to technique and color and contrasts.

"You're really good at this, Tenley."

"Be careful!" Tenley warned. "Don't smudge them. Here, come here." She waved Pennie over to the window and pushed out her screen, something she'd clearly done before. "Hold both of your hands like this."

"What are you doing?"

"Just do it," Tenley said, forcing Pennie's palms flat and yanking them out the window.

Tenley blew a quick breath. A gust of air swirled around Pennie's hands. "Tenley! Stop!" Pennie pulled her hands back.

127

"It's just wind. What are you so afraid of?" Tenley put the screen in place again.

"It's not *just wind*. This is exactly why I'm here. You need to *stop doing this*."

Tenley grabbed her phone. "Okay, look. I'm sorry that for some reason I can make the wind blow. It's weird, I know. But it's also awesome. I'm not hurting anybody. I'm just drying my nails and stuff. So I don't know why you have to go and get all freaked out about it."

"Because." Pennie lowered her voice. "Every time you create wind, you're putting yourself in danger." She tapped on her temple, careful not to smudge her nails. The hologram form appeared in front of her. "You need to sign this."

But Tenley wasn't looking. "You're kidding!" She shook her phone. "This is not possible. It didn't record! The whole tutorial. We have to start all over again." She threw her phone across the desk and slumped into her chair with her back to Pennie.

Pennie sat down on the bed. When she did, the hologram disappeared. "This is serious, Tenley. We only have—" She looked at the clock on the bedside table and did a quick calculation. "Thirty-five hours and fifty-one minutes—"

"That's how long I have until the nomination?" Now Tenley was distracted *and* panicked. She held her cell phone up to Pennie.

"Don't record this, please."

"I'm seeing if it works." She fumbled with her phone. "This is really weird."

"You know what happened in the mall. With the rock?"

Pennie went to the window and shut it.

"It wasn't me," Tenley said. "Give me your hands. I have to take the polish off."

Pennie held out her fingers while Tenley wiped her nails clean. "It *was* you. Maybe you didn't exactly mean for it to happen, but it was you."

"I put the rock back, Pennie. Someone else must have thrown it at those girls."

"Listen, Tenley. You have the power to create a very powerful wind, which is one of the four weather elements. I should have stopped you from using it a long time ago, but I didn't. And now, something very bad is going to happen to both of us if you keep using it."

"Girls?" Mrs. Tylwyth called from the top of the stairs. "I've made some lemon squares. And I've saved the spoons for you?"

"No thanks, Mom. I'm having recording problems." Tenley, finished with the last nail, dropped Pennie's hand.

"Pennie?" Mrs. Tylwyth stuck her head inside the doorway, holding a wooden spoon with yellow dough on it. "Would you like the spoon?"

"Yes, she would," Tenley answered. "I have homework, too."

"Pennie dear, why don't we leave Tenley alone. Come downstairs. I saved a little more in the bowl."

"She'd love to," Tenley said.

Pennie sighed.

"I'd love to, Mrs. Tylwyth." Pennie stood and followed her down the stairs.

24

Ten years, one month and six days earlier
Hadley Beach

Halloween. Three year-old Tenley is running down a sidewalk dressed as Snow White. She trips on the cement and her bag of candy spills out into the street. Tenley begins to cry but stops when she sees her mother is distracted by another mother up ahead. She narrows her toddler eyes and concentrates, blowing out a quick breath. Immediately, a wind tunnel forms over the candy and quickly vacuums it all up. Tenley blows at another quick breath and holds her bag open for the candy to drop back inside. She runs to catch up with her mother who is pulling a red wagon filled with more candy.

***

Eight years, seven months and nineteen days earlier
Hadley Beach

Tenley's mother peeks her head into the bedroom just as Tenley makes her first mark on the wall. "Oh no, honey. We don't draw on walls. Only paper. Remember we talked about that the last time, how that makes Mommy and Gerty sad because we have to clean it all up and paint it again?" Tenley nods and returns her blue marker to her drawing table. "Good girl," Mrs. Tylwyth smiles and disappears.

As soon as she's gone, a look spreads across little Tenley's face. She stands with all the markers and goes to the wall again.

A few minutes later, the wall looks like a subway stop. Lines and squiggles cross over themselves in every color as high as a five-year-old's arm can reach. Tenley continues scribbling until her mom's voice trills up the stairs. "Tenley? Time to go now."

Little Tenley drops her markers. She hurries to the bathroom, fills her glass with water, and returns to the wall. Then she throws the water into the air and blows out a quick breath.

The wind catches the water, sending it splashing against the wall. Another quick breath from her gets the water swirling and scrubbing the mess clean.

Finally, Tenley blows out a long steady stream of air, which dries the wall like an industrial strength blower. When the wall is a perfect white again, Tenley runs out the door.

132

***

Pennie opened her eyes. She'd been dreaming.

It took a moment for her to remember where she was and why she felt like she was pinned down to the couch. Earth. Gravity. Time.

She pulled the blanket off and rolled herself up to sitting.

Last night, Tenley and Mrs. Tylwyth had stayed up to watch America's Next Most Inspirational Teen reruns. Pennie had been so exhausted she'd finally excused herself and come into the living room to nap. Except she must have slept through the night.

Her shoes were off. She pushed herself up to standing. Had Mrs. Tylwyth noticed her small feet? Right now, she could barely move them at all. She felt like she was fighting her way through sludge, just like she had yesterday when she'd first landed in the tree. She shuffled her way over to the doorway where she could see the clock on the kitchen stove. 5:30 a.m.

Pennie paused. It didn't sound like anyone was up yet. Going to Tenley and having her sign the form before she was fully awake was an option, Pennie thought. She might even think she was dreaming. Except if Pennie scared her by mistake, Tenley would shriek loud enough for Mrs. Tylwyth to rush in. And then Pennie would have to explain what she was doing, lurking around in Tenley's room.

133

Pennie shuffled around again and went to the window. The sky! It was the most beautiful color she'd ever seen. Not quite pink and not quite orange. She thought of Tink's paintings and wondered if she'd ever seen the sunrise from Earth before.

A lump formed in her throat. Pennie wouldn't be seeing too many sunrises at all if she couldn't get Tenley to give up her element in the next twenty-six hours and thirty minutes. She'd be looking at gray walls inside the Administrative buildings. For eternity.

She had a new worry now, too. There was no doubt about what she'd seen at the mall yesterday; Tenley had used her element to throw that rock. If she kept using her wind to move objects around in public, it was only a matter of time before Mother Nature would find her.

The thought made Pennie's eyes heavy. Maybe she'd just lie down again for a spell. She shuffled back to the couch. With heavy arms, she twisted her long red hair into a bun, fluffed up the pillow, and plopped down.

25

24:00:00
Hadley Beach

Holden picked himself up. The ramp must have been wet. There was no other reason he would have lost his balance and tumbled into the street like that.

"Not such a great idea with a cast on," a teacher with a stack of books warned. "How 'bout we don't try that again."

"Sure thing, Mr. Lombarto." Holden waved. Mr. Lombarto continued down the path into Hadley Middle School.

Holden scanned the drop-off zone for any more teachers who might be watching. Instead, he spotted a girl in tennis whites by the crosswalk. She waved at someone behind him. He looked back to make sure it wasn't a teacher, or any other kind of adult, then hopped back on his skateboard again and headed to the ramp.

"Hey, Casper, courts are that way," a boy on a scooter yelled.

135

Holden couldn't hear the tennis girl's response under the rumble of his wheels but he hoped it was something equally annoying. That kid was always harassing other kids from his scooter, then zooming off.

"Holden!"

It was the tennis girl. He must have been hearing things.

"Hey, *Holden*."

This time he stopped.

"How do you know my name?" he shouted across the street.

"Your uncle. We're friends."

"You're friends with my uncle? That's like, a little weird. He's old."

"I mean we're not *friends*, friends. We work ... *out* in the same place."

"K, that's still weird," Holden mumbled.

Pennie started across the crosswalk.

Gravity felt a little easier on her since going back to sleep again this morning. Or maybe it was Mrs. Tylwyth's chocolate chip waffles. She'd had six. If she lived on Earth, she'd eat waffles for breakfast, lunch, and dinner.

"Are you on the tennis team?" Holden asked.

Pennie stepped onto the sidewalk and shook her head, confused.

"Oh, cuz your skirt, it's like a tennis one."

Mrs. Tylwyth had insisted on buying Pennie three pairs of jeans at the mall but this morning they'd all itched so badly Pennie had looked for a skirt to borrow instead. Tenley's old tennis skirt was the only one that fit her.

"Do you go to school here?" Holden asked.

She half nodded. "I'm new."

He frowned. "But it's the end of the school year?"

Pennie stared at Holden. He had a kind face, and his eyes were a deep brown. Although Laraby, like most Fair Ones, didn't know which power his client possessed—and wouldn't know until Holden turned eighteen—Pennie could tell he was going to be a strong force against Mother Nature someday.

Holden mistook Pennie's intense stare to be that of terror. The girl had it rough, he thought. What kind of parents would make their kid start a new school at the end of the year, *in a tennis skirt*?

"So, do you know *anyone* here?" Holden asked.

"I know Tenley."

"Tenley Tylwyth?" He lifted up his skateboard. The ramp would have to wait. "Yeah, I know her." He looked down at his cast.

"You tried to stop that Frisbee."

"Whatever."

"That was really nice of you."

Holden felt his cheeks burn. This girl was good-looking in a whole different way from Tenley Tylwyth. Shy and sweet and kind of Tinkerbell-ish.

The bell rang.

"What's your name, anyway?" Holden asked as they started toward the school together.

"It's Pennie. One."

"Where are you from, Pennie One?"

"Up north."

137

"Well, welcome to Hadley Middle School. Home of the Hedgehog." He pointed toward the front entrance, a sculpture of a hedgehog above it.

Across the grounds, another student was walking toward the entrance. It was Tenley, who'd gone off to take some selfies before school.

"That's the Tenley Tylwyth you're friends with? The one who wants to get on that TV show?"

"*America's Next Most Inspiration Teen*. That's her."

"Are you trying to get on it too?"

"No. My mom was her babysitter."

The second bell rang.

"Well, if she's too busy texting and stuff to help you out," he shrugged. "I'm pretty much always around."

"Thanks."

"Coming in?" He waited at the entrance.

"In a minute."

"Better not be late. Frimpy hates late." Holden looked back at Tenley. "And don't wait for her. She always gets in trouble."

Pennie heard it first—the rumbling. Next, a strong gust of wind blew past her, ruffling up her tennis skirt. Behind her, someone started shrieking. It was Tenley, flying through the air.

"Help!" Tenley screamed.

Holden sprinted toward her.

Tenley was too high off the ground for anyone to do anything but watch as she flew head-on for a maple tree. Just before impact, her body jerked to a stop.

Her sash had caught on a branch.

"Are you okay?" Holden yelled up to her.

"No!"

The sash was starting to rip.

"One of you, call for help!" Holden shouted to a group of students who'd run over.

"Like 911?"

"And you!" He pointed to another student. "Get Frimpy."

Pennie looked up at Tenley; she was helpless without her tools. "Hang on, Tenley!"

Holden spread his arms out below her. "Don't worry. I'll catch you."

The sash tore through. Tenley plummeted downward. Just before dropping on top of Holden, another gust of wind swept her straight up again. This time, she stayed suspended in the air for a moment before gently dropping feet first next to Holden.

"Are you *okay*? What just happened?" he asked.

Pennie knew exactly what had happened. She gave Tenley a knowing look. Except this time, it had saved her life.

"That was like *awful*. Did anyone get it on video? I need to post it immediately."

"I did." A boy held up his phone.

"Yes!" Tenley fist-pumped. "Put: 'ANMIT nominee survives a near-death experience' on it. Don't forget to hashtag ANMIT."

"Move it, people." Principal Frimpy broke through the crowd. "What just happened here? And get it right the first time or you'll all meet me in my office."

A tall boy with large glasses spoke up. "She almost flew into that tree."

139

Principal Frimpy sighed. "It's going to get painfully hot in my office, people."

"It's true," a girl chimed in. "That sash got caught in a branch and saved her."

"This?" Mr. Frimpy picked up the ripped sash. "You're telling me this thing stopped Ms. Tylwyth from hitting the tree?"

Yups all around.

Mr. Frimpy handed the sash back to Tenley. "Can you walk, Miss Tylwyth?"

"I think so."

"Good. Pulling silly pranks like this is not the way to get your nomination, Ms. Tylwyth. It's a way to get you disqualified. Come with me."

"Disqualified? It wasn't a prank, Principal Frimpy. I swear."

"Really? Then what was it?"

Tenley pointed at Pennie. "*She* did it. This new girl is trying to kill me!"

Pennie froze. "What?"

"Who are you, then?" Principal Frimpy looked at her.

"She's the stalker. Remember, she fainted yesterday?"

"Oh yes," Principal Frimpy said. "How could I forget?"

"I don't know how she did it, Principal Frimpy," Tenley started to cry. "But she was warning me about weird things, telling me bad stuff was going to happen. And then this gust of wind picked me up and flew me into the tree. Now I need a new sash."

"Hold it." Holden stepped forward. "This new girl didn't do anything. She was just standing here like the rest of us."

140

Principal Frimpy studied him. "Mr. Wonderbolt would have no reason to lie, would he?"

Holden shook his head. "She's not a stalker, Principal Frimpy. She's Tenley's babysitter's daughter."

"I see. Mrs. Tylwyth has been calling all morning about getting her enrolled." He clapped quickly. "People, get to class. Except for you, Ms. Tylwyth. You'll need to get checked out by the nurse first. Would anyone like to escort Ms. Tylwyth?"

The students picked up their paces and ran off.

"I can help, sir," Dan Ringer said.

"Hello, son." Principal Frimpy brightened. "I didn't know you were here."

"Hi, Danny." Tenley batted her eyelashes at him.

He ignored her and turned to Pennie. "Hey there, Pennie. Nice to see you again."

Pennie stood confused. Had she told him her name?

"You're looking much better than yesterday."

He was the teenager who'd brought her to the nurse's station, Pennie realized. "Thanks. I'm feeling much better."

"Glad to hear it," Dan smiled.

"I think I'm going to faint," Tenley cried, placing the back of her hand on her forehead.

Dan rushed over and swooped her up in his arms. Holden stole a look at Pennie. She seemed as enamored of Dan as all the other girls were. *Figures,* he thought. Dan was twice his size, in every direction.

Tenley took a few selfies in Dan's arms on the way into school.

141

"As for you, Pennie, is it?"

Pennie answered Principal Frimpy with a nod.

"You'll need to come to the office with me. I'm afraid I'm going to have to send you home with some papers to sign before we can get you enrolled."

Principal Frimpy started into the building. Holden and Pennie followed.

"See you later, I guess," Holden said.

"Yeah. See you later."

"Oh hey!" Holden said. "Do you skateboard?"

Pennie shook her head.

"I'll teach you, then. See ya." He disappeared down the hall.

"Come along, Miss One," Principal Frimpy called from his doorway. "I've already wasted enough time this morning."

Pennie looked at the clock on the wall and sighed. So had she.

26

22:00:00
Hadley Beach

By the time Pennie rounded the Tylwyths' driveway, she was sure of it: Mother Nature had discovered Tenley. She might not have captured her today, but she'd be back. A rogue gust of wind wasn't the only weather weapon she had, either. Tenley wasn't safe anywhere now.

Pennie tried the front door. "*Today* it's locked?"

She sat on the front steps and looked up at the late morning sky. Birds were chirping and leaves were rustling. Mother Nature was terrifying but it was obvious why she would do anything to protect her planet. The Earth was electric and, except for gravity, magical, even.

A giant object dropped in front of her.

"*Gavron!*" Pennie jumped to her feet.

"Howdy-do, Fairly One. Didn't mean to scare ya." He brushed

143

down his sooty robes. "This place gives me the willies. Look at all this *nature*."

Pennie poked his shoulder.

"Can you tell I've been working out?" Gavron winked.

"No, but I know you're not a hologram now. What are you *doing* here?"

"I think you mean to say, 'How was your trip, you handsome young thing?'"

Pennie crossed her arms. Gavron certainly wasn't a young thing. He'd been around for a few centuries at least. "Come on, Gavron. Mrs. Tylwyth could be back any second now."

"Here's the deal." He held up the purple dinosaur stopwatch. "This thing's no good."

"You came all the way here to complain about *this*?" Tenley could show up any second, too. It wouldn't be the first time she'd left school early.

"I don't think you heard me right, Fairly One." Gavron stepped closer. "This thing doesn't *do* anything. It just ticks down numbers. It's probably not even real Fair Force equipment."

"It's a stopwatch, Gavron. You're the one who wanted it."

"Well now I want something else."

"I'm a little lacking in the tool department."

Gavron dropped his eyes to the tennis skirt. "I *like* these updated robes. Very risqué. I'm pretty sure the F Force will give you dress code for them, though."

"Leave, Gavron."

"Did I not make myself clear? I'm not leaving until I get a fair trade. The boys and I—"

Three drops of drool splashed onto Pennie's pink shoe. Three filthy sipLips waved down from the roof.

"We risked our lives to bring you here, Fair One. Don't break the code."

"What code?"

"The code that says if you don't get me something better than *this*." He tossed the stopwatch at her. "I'll conveniently forget not to drop a few bits of meteor shrapnel onto your client's head one day."

Mrs. Tylwyth's car turned into the driveway.

"I told you," Pennie panicked. "You have to go."

Gavron activated his propellers but Pennie grabbed his arm. "Wait. Don't. She'll see you."

"I'm out of here. They're barbarians."

"If she sees you, she'll tell others about you, and they'll tell others, and eventually someone's Fair One will hear about it and they'll tell the Fair Force, and then *you* will be arrested."

Gavron's eyes bugged. He looked up at the sipLips and deactivated his propellers.

"Just *look* human." Pennie told him. "And don't talk."

The car stopped in front of the garage. "And who's this?" Mrs. Tylwyth asked, stepping out.

Gavron froze.

"My salesman friend," Pennie said, remembering the stopwatch and strapping it around her wrist.

Mrs. Tylwyth considered Gavron's robes. "What are you selling?"

"Stroons," Pennie answered.

"Stroons?"

Gavron shifted his eyes over to Mrs. Tylwyth, who happened to be quite fond of cutlery. She smiled at him warmly. He looked away quickly.

"A cross between a straw and a spoon," Pennie answered.

"How clever. I'd love to see your stroons."

"And he'd love to show them to you. Right, *Gavron*?" Gavron remained frozen. He didn't just dislike humans; he was *terrified* of them.

"He's shy, Mrs. Tylwyth," Pennie apologized. "And missing a lot of teeth."

That seemed to be enough of an explanation for Mrs. Tylwyth. "I don't like dentists myself," she said with a wave of her hand. "Perhaps another day. Do you have a card, then?"

Gavron didn't respond.

"And he's hard of hearing. Right, Gavron?"

"Poor thing." Mrs. Tylwyth unlocked the door and stepped into the house. "I need to get you a key, dear. Is Tenley home early, too? When Principal Frimpy called about getting you registered he mentioned she had some sort of incident at school."

"I think she had some trouble posting a selfie. I'm pretty sure she's fine now, Mrs. Tylwyth."

"Good. I'm going to print out the school forms. I'd love to see those stroons of yours." Mrs. Tylwyth smiled at Gavron and closed the door behind her.

"Okay, go! Get out of here, Gavron," Pennie waved.

"The thing is, Fairly One," he whispered. "I can't leave

146

empty-handed. I don't want my boys thinking I'm some kind of pushover."

"Fine," Pennie said. She walked to the driver's side of the car and opened it. "How about this?" She held up the garage door opener.

"What does it do?"

"*This*."

The garage door slid up.

"And *this*," Pennie said, shutting it again. "If I give it to you, will you leave?"

"A wall opener," Gavron mumbled, transfixed. "Lots of walls in Fair City we'd like to open, right, boys?"

The sipLips snorted.

"So. Deal?" Pennie asked.

"Deal." Gavron snatched the door opener from her. "Let's roll, boys." He slipped the garage door opener in his pocket and narrowed his eyes at Pennie. "How's it going down here, anyway, Fairly One? Your gravity-groper behaving?"

Pennie's face betrayed her. "It's harder than I thought, to be honest."

"That is a sad, sad story. Tell you what. I'm offering you a free ride home. Right now. Whaddya say? Go on a quick space picnic with me before the F Force does whatever it is they're going to do to you. You won't regret it."

At that very moment, it was tempting.

Mrs. Tylwyth cranked open the kitchen window. "Say, do you sell sporks too?"

"Just stroons," Pennie answered.

Mrs. Tylwyth looked a little sorry about it and cranked the window closed.

Pennie's heart sank. She couldn't leave now. Mrs. Tylwyth didn't deserve to lose a daughter. As Lady Fairship had explained, all memories of anyone who knew Tenley would be erased and it was awful to think of Mrs. Tylwyth alone.

"I can't go yet," Pennie told Gavron.

He shrugged. "Suit yourself. They're all doomed anyway. Mama N's getting ready to do some major renovations around here. With or without a Fairly One to protect them, all these gravity-gropers are going to get flat-out *smoked*."

"Hey, Pennie!" Holden waved from the end of the driveway.

"Oh no," Pennie said. "Gavron, you have to go!"

He activated his propellers.

"Behind the garage." She pointed. "Go. Now."

Gavron looked back as he hurried away. "We could have made beautiful filth together, Fairly One. See ya'."

A moment later, inside a swirling vortex, the sipLips shot up into the sky.

"See ya," Pennie whispered, wondering if she hadn't just made the second biggest mistake of her life.

27

21:30:32
Hadley Beach

"Hey, Pennie. I hope it's okay I came over. I brought my extra." Holden held up a second skateboard with his good arm and skated up the driveway. "You said you wanted to learn to board so I figured now's a good time."

"Did I say that?" Pennie asked. "I'm not sure now's a good time, Holden. How did you get out of school?"

"Normally I'd be at PE right now, but," he pointed to his cast, "I have to go to the doctor later, so my mom let me get out."

"It's really nice of you to come over. The thing is, I was in the middle of doing something for school."

"There's no homework 'cause of the field trip tomorrow, right?"

Mrs. Tylwyth cranked the window open again. "Pennie, dear? Another salesman?"

"No, Mrs. Tylwyth. This is Holden, from school."

"Hi," Holden waved.

"Oh hello, young man. Are you a friend of Tenley's too?"

Holden gave Pennie a look. "Kind of, I guess."

"Lemonade?"

"No, thank you," Holden answered.

"Holden just came over to teach me how to skateboard."

"Well, that's nice," Mrs. Tylwyth said. "I've always wanted to learn how to do that myself. Go on, have fun!"

She closed the window.

"Pretty normal mom," Holden said. "What happened to Tenley?"

"What do you mean?"

"Sorry. I keep forgetting you're friends with her. She's just a little *into* herself." Holden dropped the extra board. "Ready?"

"Trust me, I'm not good at gravity-related things. I'll just watch."

"You look pretty coordinated to me." Holden held out his hand. "Step on."

Pennie placed a pink high-top gingerly on the board. "I can't do it," she said, stepping off. This morning, she'd balled up some socks and shoved them inside each shoe to make them fit better. But they weren't going to help her balance any better on her tiny feet.

"Come on. YOLO and stuff," Holden insisted.

Pennie set one foot onto the skateboard again. Then the other.

"That's it. Let's go!" Holden led her down the driveway

slowly. He picked up speed halfway down. Pennie yelped a few times but managed to stay on.

At the end, Pennie jumped off and flopped over. Learning to use her propellers had been less terrifying.

"See?" Holden winced, shaking out the hand Pennie had been clutching. "You did it. Okay, now again, and this time without me holding on." He swept up the board with his good arm. "That's a cool necklace, by the way."

Pennie stood quickly. The crystal eight had fallen out of her shirt. "Thanks." She tucked it back in again.

"Is it an eternity sign or an eight?"

"An eight, I think. Fine." Pennie changed the subject quickly. "I'll try it again."

"Awesome." Holden started up the driveway. "You'll get it this time. I bet you're great at everything you do." He blushed.

Pennie struggled to keep up with him. "I'm not at all. But thanks, you're a really sweet boy."

"*Boy*?" Holden was offended.

"Boy-*guy*," she corrected herself.

Holden still looked insulted.

"And strong too. Trying to save Tenley from the Frisbee like that."

He stopped. "If you were there, how come I never saw you?"

A car honked behind them. The passenger door opened and Tenley stepped out.

"Principal Frimpy told me I could come home. My mom didn't answer her phone. So I Ubered." She shut the door and walked toward them. "What's your excuse, skate boarder?"

Holden held up his cast. "Doctor's appointment."

Satisfied, she walked to Pennie.

"Look, Pennie. I'm sorry about saying all that stuff to Principal Frimpy. It's just that everything was fine before you showed up and now look at me." She pointed to a scratch across her forehead. "How am I going to go on camera with this?" She didn't wait for the answer. She walked past them and hurried in the front door.

Pennie turned to Holden. "You better go."

"Maybe we can stay after school tomorrow and practice?"

"Sure," Pennie said. She couldn't look him in the eye. She wouldn't be here after school tomorrow.

"All right. Later." Holden jumped on his board and waved as he flew down the driveway with the second skateboard tucked under his arm.

Pennie checked the stopwatch, happy to have it back. **21:10:05**. She hurried to the front door and stepped inside.

"I hope ravioli is okay for dinner tonight. It might be too Italian for Tenley but it's one of my specialties," Mrs. Tylwyth said from the stove.

"Sounds perfect, Mrs. Tylwyth."

"Pennie, why don't you call me Sylma."

Tenley walked into the kitchen. "Mom, did you get my text? About my sash?"

"We'll get you a new one, honey. I just haven't had a single second today. We had a shipment of the most glorious chairs. Red velvet, in perfect shape. Gold arms, not a single scratch."

"Okay." Tenley nodded, disappointed.

"How about we go after I finish Pennie's paperwork."

"Please don't go to any trouble for me, Mrs. Tylwyth."

"*Sylma.* Don't be silly, Pennie. It's the least we could do for Gerty. You're family now."

Pennie smiled weakly.

"Come on, Pennie," Tenley said. "Let's redo the tribal nail art video." She walked out of the kitchen and up the stairs.

Mrs. Tylwyth handed Pennie a piece of paper. "This is your permission slip for tomorrow's field trip. Why they'd have you all go so early, I can't imagine. Anyway, just hand it to your teacher, he knows it's late."

"Thank you, Mrs. Tylwyth."

"Sylma."

"Sylma."

Mrs. Tylwyth deflated suddenly. "Pennie, did Gerty ever mention Mr. Tylwyth's letters?"

"Yes," Pennie said softly.

Mrs. Tylwyth hesitated. "They're not really from him."

Pennie nodded.

"It's probably time I told her," Mrs. Tylwyth said.

"Probably," Pennie agreed.

Something crashed upstairs. "*Omigod,*" Tenley yelled. "I just broke a nail! I'm going to be a *monster* at the nominations!"

"On the other hand," Pennie said. "What's the harm in waiting another day or two?"

Mrs. Tylwyth smiled sadly. "I think Tenley should know the truth before the nominations, just in case she's hoping he might be watching. He's never coming back for us, I'm afraid." She walked over to the stairs. "Tenley, dear, let's go get that sash now. We need a little mother-daughter time."

Tenley appeared at the top. "What about Pennie?"

"She's going to stay here. Maybe start researching Hadley Beach a little?" She turned back to Pennie. "Now that you'll be living here?"

"Great idea," Pennie said weakly.

28

15:15:20
Hadley Beach

"Is she dead?"

"Of course not. She's snoring, honey."

Tenley dropped down to the grass to inspect Pennie. "Why would she fall asleep out here? There are like, *bugs*."

"Pennie?" Mrs. Tylwyth shook her gently. "Pennie. Wake up, dear."

Pennie opened her eyes. Her left cheek was pressed into something cold and itchy. She pushed herself up on her elbows. "Hi. I was trying to see if I could watch the grass grow. I guess I fell asleep." She checked to make sure Tink's necklace was still tucked inside her shirt before getting to her knees.

"I'm sorry we were gone for so long." Mrs. Tylwyth helped Pennie to her feet. "We had a little incident driving back from the sash store."

"Lightning! Crashed right in front of us and took down a tree. It was legit insane," Tenley said.

Mrs. Tylwyth looked exhausted. "It took two hours for the fire department to remove the tree. We tried to call you, Pennie. But we didn't have your number."

"Do you even have a phone?"

"Did you say, *lightning*?" Pennie rubbed her cheek.

"We called the house phone like a bazillion times too," Tenley said. "But I guess you were out here watching the grass grow. Which is completely normal." Tenley rolled her eyes.

Pennie checked the stopwatch. **15:09:19.**

"It's almost five o'clock already," Mrs. Tylwyth said. "I haven't even started dinner yet. Let's get you hungry girls inside." Mrs. Tylwyth led Pennie up to the front door. Just before they stepped inside, the sky lit up and crashed behind them. Another flash of lightning barely missed Tenley.

***

After dinner—and Mrs. Tylwyth was right, her ravioli was delicious—Tenley excused herself to go set up the nail tutorial.

"Hurry up, Pennie, we're running out of time," she yelled down from the stairs.

They were definitely running out of time.

Pennie finished helping Mrs. Tylwyth clear the table. "Thank you for dinner, Mrs. Tylwyth. I won't ever forget it."

156

"Well, I'll make it again for you, Pennie. And listen," she lowered her voice at the sink. "I told Tenley about her father's letters. She claims she knew I was the one writing them all along. I'm not sure she wasn't just saying that, but I didn't want to press it. I thought you should know in case she brings it up."

"That's great, Mrs. Tylwyth."

"Sylma. I feel so much better. It's like a weight has been lifted off my shoulders. I didn't realize how exhausting it was to carry around such a big secret."

"I know what you mean," Pennie said quietly.

"Now go on up and help Tenley," Mrs. Tylwyth said.

Pennie thanked her again and climbed the stairs.

"You still have your nail tips on, right?" Tenley asked as soon as Pennie entered the room.

"I'm leaving tomorrow."

Tenley spun around. "*What*? Why? Have you told my mom?"

"No."

"Okay, well, can you wait to tell her until *after* the nominations?"

"Tenley—"

"Good. Thanks." Tenley turned away to set her cell phone up against a stack of books. "There. It's gotta record this time." She yanked Pennie over and began inspecting her nail tips.

Out the window, Pennie spotted a falling star. On Earth, a falling star lasted a millisecond, but in Fair City it lit the place up for a day or two. Even the grumpiest of Administrators brightened when they saw one.

"Listen, Tenley. I'm not who you think I am."

157

"A ginger?"

"One of you."

"Popular?"

"From Earth."

Tenley dropped Pennie's hands and lined up her nail tools. "As in *this* Earth, the one I'm standing on?"

"Yes, this Earth. I'm not supposed to be telling you any of this." Pennie sat on Tenley's bed.

"Are you okay? Do you need to take another nap or something? I guess I can prop you up against the wall. I'm going to need your hands, though."

"I'm fine. It's just the gravity."

"Right." Tenley said, busy rearranging the polish. "The gravity."

"Tenley, I'm a Fair One." There, she'd said it. She looked out the window again, expecting the Fair Force to drop down and arrest her on the spot.

"A fair *one*?"

"You'd know us as Fairies. What we were before."

Tenley stopped fiddling with the nail supplies. "Okay, so wait. You're saying you're a fairy?"

"Shh. I don't want your mom to know. Or anyone else. No one else can know this or I can get into a lot of trouble."

"Where are your wings?" Tenley whispered.

"We don't use them anymore. Those were our ancestors."

"How do you get around?"

"Propellers."

"Like a helicopter?"

"Exactly."

"So where are those?"

"I didn't bring them. Or my tools, which don't work here."

"On Earth?"

"Right."

Tenley put her hands on her hips and considered. "Are you for realsies?"

"Yes. For realsies. I swear."

"Fine." Tenley grabbed her phone and hurried over to the window. "Is there like the mother ship out there?" she whispered, holding her phone up to the sky.

Pennie hesitated. "I thought letting you use your element early was doing my job really well. But it's not. It's put you in danger." Pennie stood and showed Tenley the stopwatch. **12:30:09.** "This is counting down how much time we have left before something bad happens."

Tenley's eyes narrowed. "A purple dinosaur? Really?"

"It's made to look like human technology."

"That's insulting, I guess. What kind of something bad?"

"There's *a certain someone* trying to obliterate you, all of you."

"Principal Frimpy?"

"This is serious, Tenley. You have until 8:00 a.m. tomorrow to sign an agreement saying you will stop using your wind element or you don't even want to know what will happen to you."

"I'll be disqualified?"

"You'll be ... not here anymore."

"Okay. So let me get this straight. What you're telling me

is that if I don't agree to stop making a little breeze once in a while, then tomorrow at 8:00 a.m., I'm going to be destroyed by Principal Frimpy?"

"By someone much worse."

"Who?"

"Mother Nature."

Tenley crossed her arms. "Okay, you see how that makes *no sense*, right? That's not a real person."

"She's not a person, but she *is* real. And she doesn't want you or anyone else able to control the weather."

"Why isn't she after you?"

"Because I don't have weather powers, Tenley. Only you do. Did. Soon."

Tenley sat down on her bed.

"All you want me to do is tell you that I'll stop with the wind? Fine. I'll stop."

"And you need to sign this." Pennie tapped on her temple.

When the hologram form appeared, Tenley pushed herself off the bed so fast she tripped. "Omigod. How did you do that?" She poked it.

"It's part of our Intel. It's a chip. Manuals and forms. Boring things. After you sign, you won't be able to use your element again. Ever."

Tenley took a step back. "So what's in it for me?"

"What?"

"What do *I* get out of it?"

"You *have* to sign this form otherwise you'll be—you'll go away."

"Where?"

Pennie tapped on her temple again. "It says it here in the fine print."

Tenley stepped up to the second hologram and squinted. "I'm not reading all this. It's tiny."

"I know. Basically, it says that if you don't sign this, you get erased."

"Like a photo?"

Pennie looked sorry about it when she nodded.

"Erased as in *dead*?"

"And we don't want that to happen."

"*Yeah* we don't want that to happen." Her phone pinged in rapid succession. "No!" She crumpled to the ground.

Pennie rushed to her side. "Does something hurt?"

"I've lost thirteen followers. I'm never going to get the nomination now. *Never*." She showed the phone to Pennie. "Every ANMIT contestant has more followers than me. Even the little genius kid who builds electric rockets for his gerbils. Even *he* has more followers."

Pennie turned back to the hologram forms still hovering in the air. "Tenley. Please. Sign this."

"Have you no *mercy*? I'm in a serious *crisis* here. Take your cool little hologram tricks and show them to genius gerbil boy instead. I'm sure he could find a way to put them in every household in Hadley Beach."

Tenley froze.

"Omigod."

She blinked at Pennie.

161

"O-*mi*-god."

"What?"

Tenley pointed to the holograms. "*Can* you beam one of these things into every house in Hadley Beach?"

"What?"

"Vote for me, Tenley T!" She raised her arms. "On a hologram billboard *in every* living room *in every* house in Hadley Beach!"

"I don't have that Intel."

"So program it. *Anything* can be programmed, *Pennie*."

"I don't have the access to do that." Pennie looked out the window again.

"I'll sign the form."

Pennie blinked at her. "You will?"

"Give me a pen."

"Just sign with your finger. Right here."

Tenley lifted an eyebrow. "And you'll send a hologram ad into every house in Hadley Beach? Tomorrow night at seven forty-five, fifteen minutes before the vote? Promise?"

That would be eleven hours and forty-five minutes *after* Tenley had been erased if she didn't sign the form. So yes, Pennie would promise anything.

"Okay, but just so you understand, Tenley. You can't use your element ever again, starting now. No wind. No matter what."

"And just so *you* understand, all I've *ever* wanted to be is America's Next Most Inspirational Teen. I'd give up *everything* to get it."

"Then it's a deal."

They shook on it.

Tenley signed the hologram.

"There's no *way* I can lose now." Tenley grinned. "Right?"

"Right." Pennie grinned back.

29

2:00:00
Hadley Beach

"Wake up!" Tenley nudged Pennie. "We're can't be late. Mr. Mingby's gonna leave us if we're not there by seven."

Pennie sat up.

"I left some clothes for you on the bed. You cannot wear this tennis outfit again."

Tenley walked out of the living room and Pennie looked down at the stopwatch. Two hours until the Fair Force arrived. She stood quickly.

And plopped back down again.

Tenley had signed the form! Which meant today, her last two hours on Earth, she could relax. She'd done it; The Right to Delete. The rest of it was up to the Fair Force. All she needed to do now was get Tenley away from as many people as possible

164

when they arrived.

Pennie strutted into the kitchen. Even gravity felt like her friend this morning.

Sitting at the table, ignoring the eggs in front of her, Tenley was playing with her phone.

"Pennie." Mrs. Tylwyth yawned by the sink. "We were worried you'd sleep right through the field trip this morning. Tenley tried to wake you three times."

"Four," Tenley corrected her.

"Four." Mrs. Tylwyth opened the refrigerator. "Honestly, a field trip at seven in the morning."

"Mr. Mingby said it's because the tickets were half price or something if you went this early." Tenley shrugged. "And we're a public school so we're lucky to even have pencils."

"You all brought in your own pencils this year," Mrs. Tylwyth said. "They cut the pencil budget."

"Right. See?"

Pennie sat at the table.

"Now, Pennie, we've been discussing a new bed for you. We were thinking we could put two beds in Tenley's room. Weren't we, Tenley, dear?"

"Yup."

"Please, Mrs. Tylwyth, don't buy a new bed for me. I'm fine on the couch, really."

"Who said anything about buy? I own an antique store, dear. I've got dozens of beds to pick from. And it's *Sylma*." Mrs. Tylwyth placed a plate of eggs and a glass of orange juice in front of her. "Now, do you have the permission slip I gave you?

Mr. Mingby's a stickler for that kind of thing."

"Agreed," Tenley said.

"I have it. Thank you." Pennie took a sip of the juice. This would be her last real orange juice, not the instant orange mix they had in Fair City.

Tenley groaned.

"Tenley, you're still having trouble with your phone?"

"It's gotta be the Internet, Mom. I'm telling you, nothing is posting to my YouTube. Nothing."

"I'll make a call from work," Mrs. Tylwyth said.

Tenley leaned into Pennie. "Wait, Pennie. Do you need the Internet for the, *you know*, thing we discussed that will happen at seven forty-five tonight?"

"No." Pennie said quietly. "Not necessary."

"Good. Hey, Mom, you can forget about putting my flyers up at the store today. Pennie and I have a *much* better plan."

"Really? What is it?"

"You'll see. Right, Pen?"

Pennie smiled halfheartedly. There was no way she could create a hologram ad for Tenley without her tools. She didn't even know how to do that *with* her tools. But Laraby might, she thought. It was the least she could do for Tenley now that she'd signed the form. Once her element was properly deleted by the Fair Force, Tenley wouldn't be needing a Fair One. This would be the last thing Pennie ever did for her.

"How exciting. It's time to get going. Pennie, go on upstairs and change," Mrs. Tylwyth said.

Pennie, heavy with guilt now, stood and turned for the door.

Upstairs, a pair of skinny jeans and a light-blue T-shirt were laid out on the bed. Two light-blue sneakers (three sizes too big) were placed below. Pennie undressed and redressed quickly, tucking Tink's crystal eight under the blue shirt and stuffing socks into each shoe. She stepped into the bathroom, twisted her long red hair into a bun, and splashed cold water on her pale face. But what were these dark circles under her eyes? Gravity again, Pennie decided. It would be one thing she didn't miss back in Fair City.

Twenty minutes later, Mrs. Tylwyth's car stopped in front of the school.

"Funny. I still can't seem to find that darn garage door opener," she mumbled.

"Thanks, Mom. See ya." Tenley jumped out.

Pennie leaned over the front seat. "Mrs. Tylwyth. I just want you to know, in case I don't see you again."

Mrs. Tylwyth swatted the thought away.

"That you are a great mom."

"Well, thank you, honey."

Pennie stepped out of the car. "Good-bye, Mrs. Tylwyth."

"Sylma! And see you after school."

Pennie shut the door and waved, knowing that she wouldn't.

30

1:15:00
Hadley Beach

"**H**olden!" Pennie shouted to him as he crossed the street with his board tucked under his good arm.

"Hey, Pennie. You look so—un-tennisy." He smiled. "Not that the tennis clothes didn't look good, because those looked unreal, too." He hesitated, not knowing whether he'd just said something insulting or not. *Girls, man. The wrong words could kill you.*

A group of them, girls Pennie had never seen before, broke into a fit of giggles as they passed by.

"Hey, so, Holden," Pennie said, glancing up at the early morning sky. Not a single cloud today. It wasn't supposed to make a difference; good visibility wasn't supposed to affect the 3rdi's, but the truth was, it did. Which meant that Laraby—if he were watching them now—would see and hear everything perfectly.

"Wouldn't it be amazing if you could make a hologram? Just a simple square with some words on it, let's say?"

"That'd be cool. A hologram with *anything* on it would be cool."

They started walking.

"Right," Pennie agreed, looking at the sky. "Like let's say that you'd just gotten someone to sign a form that you *really needed them* to sign and in exchange you *promised them* a *hologram ad* that would appear at *seven forty-five* tonight in every single house in Hadley Beach?"

Holden shrugged. "Yeah, I guess. They already have some hologram stuff. I mean, like they have dead people coming back to sing on stage, which is kind of weird I guess, but whatever." At the entrance, Holden held the door for her. "Hey, wanna practice boarding again after school?"

"I can't," Pennie said.

"Tomorrow then?"

"Maybe." The back of Pennie's knees started to sweat from the lie.

"Cool."

Inside the school, it seemed like half the kids were staring at them.

"Why is everyone looking at us?" Holden whispered. "Did someone start a rumor about us going out or something?"

Pennie looked over at him. He was blushing.

Down the hall, another group of girls stood pointing at them. An entire fleet of Fair Force was less intimidating than a group of middle-school girls, Pennie thought.

Holden stopped in front of a door. "I think this is your homeroom."

Inside the classroom, a group of girls, including Tenley, turned to look at them.

"Anyway," Pennie continued. "Let's say that hologram that appeared at *seven forty-five* tonight in *every single house* in Hadley Beach read, '*Vote for Me, Tenley T, America's Next Most Inspirational Teen!*' Don't you think that would be pretty amazing? Wouldn't it be the best final thing someone could ever do for their client?"

Holden wasn't following. "I gotta go."

"Tenley might even win the nomination!" Pennie called after him.

"I think there's a better chance I'll wake up six-foot-two one morning." Holden waved, turning down the hall.

31

1:20:00
Hadley Beach

"Settle down, people. Our buses *leave* at zero-seven-hundred," Mr. Mingby, standing at the blackboard, warned everyone. "That's in twenty minutes. And when I say leave, I mean leave *you* if you're not on board. I didn't get up at the crack of dawn to be late. So I hope you all got your permission slips in." Mr. Mingby was a big burly man with surprisingly elegant glasses, which he pushed up to read the list in his hands. "If not, you'll be in homework club for the day. No exceptions."

The students went to their desks and Pennie found an empty seat in the back.

"But Mr. Mingby, what if we don't have one and it's not our fault?"

Mr. Mingby crossed his arms and looked over his glasses. "You're teenagers now. Future leaders. You, and only you, were

171

responsible for getting a parent signature. So today, you'll be staying here, Trevor. Which leaves a space open for our new student." Mr. Mingby motioned toward Pennie in the back row. "As long as you have your permission slip?"

"I've got three hundred new likes!" Tenley squealed from her desk.

"Yes, Mr. Mingby." Pennie waved the permission slip to distract his frown away from Tenley. "I've got it right here."

"Very good. See, kids. When one door closes, another one opens. That's life in a nutshell. Now. You, as seventh graders, earned this end-of-the-year field trip. Don't disappoint. Everyone but Trevor, let's go."

Tenley shrieked again. "Three hundred and *seven*."

This time, Mr. Mingby glared at her. "Excited for the theme park, are we, Ms. Tylwyth? All right, everyone, let's go!"

Outside, two yellow buses were parked along the school's curb. Tenley grabbed Pennie's elbow.

"I'm *trending*."

"Pennie One!" Holden poked Pennie's shoulder from behind. "Wanna sit with me?"

"Sure," Pennie answered.

Tenley grinned at her phone and walked away.

Students looked sleep-deprived while they waited to be told which bus they were on. A growing group of them was staring at Pennie now.

"Have you ever been to Adventures, Inc.? I've heard it's got, like, three different parks inside of it. One's all VR. Just opened," Holden said.

"VR?"

"Virtual Reality."

"Like a 3rd i," Pennie nodded, distracted by how many students were staring at her. Holden didn't answer. Pennie looked back at him quickly. "Third eye." She poked her forehead. "Virtual Reality's like a third eye, right?"

Holden shrugged. "I guess."

Mr. Mingby called off Tenley's name. She straightened her new sash and disappeared into the bus parked behind him.

After a few more names, Mr. Mingby called off Holden's name and pointed down to the second bus. Instead of heading toward it, Holden leaned into Pennie and whispered, "I'm just gonna wait here."

When the last of the names were called off, Pennie and a handful of other girls remained stranded on the grass. Mr. Mingby looked up from his clipboard.

"Any names I left off, you can get on this bus behind me."

"Excuse me, Mr. Mingby?" Holden approached him. "Would you mind if I went on this one too? Just cuz, you know, Pennie's new. And I'm assigned to show her around." He nodded toward Pennie.

Mr. Mingby skimmed through his papers, flustered. "Sure, get on, Wonderbolt."

Holden thanked him and climbed on the bus after Pennie.

The bus was packed. In the back row, Tenley was looking down at an iPad with a group of students hovering around her.

"We got the Fairy!" a girl yelled, pointing up at Pennie.

Pennie felt her cheeks drain.

"What did she say?" Holden asked.

Pennie didn't answer.

Every student was staring at her now. "Hey Fairy!" a few shouted.

"What's going on?" Holden asked.

Tenley ran down the aisle. "It must have accidentally uploaded to the Internet last night when you were telling me all that stuff!" She held out the iPad for Pennie. There was a frozen image of her standing in Tenley's room wearing the tennis outfit. "Someone's made a remix and put it on YouTube. I'm really sorry."

"You recorded everything I told you?"

"By mistake. I didn't even think our Internet was working, remember?"

"*Everything* I told you?" Pennie's voice shrilled.

"Not everything. Just this."

Tenley pressed play.

A rap montage with Pennie's image on the screen began:

"I'm not who you think I am.

A gin—gin—gin—ginger?

One of you.

Popular?

From Earth.

As in *this* Ear—ear—ear—ear—earth, the one I'm standing on?

(A huge Pennie is suddenly slipping off planet Earth)

I'm sorry, it's the gra—gra—gra—gra—gravity.

Right. The gra—gra—gra—gra—gravity.

174

OPERATION TENLEY

I'm a Fair One.

A fair *one*?

You'd know us as Fai—fai—fai—fai—fai—fai—fairies. What we
were before.

You're a fairy?

(Pennie grows huge animated wings behind her)

I don't want your mom to know. Or anyone else. I can get into
a lot of trou—

ou—ou—ou—ou—ou—ouble.

Where are your wings?

We don't use them anymore.

(The animated wings behind Pennie get crossed out and
crumble off)

How do you get around?

Propellers.

Like helicopters?

(Animated propellers appear over Pennie)

Exactly.

So where are they?

I didn't bring them to Earth.

(the propellers crumble like sand and disappear)

For rea—lsies?

Yes. For rea—rea—rea—rea—rea—rea—realsies. I swear.

(A giant animated spaceship engulfs them and takes them
away)

A lacrosse boy started singing the rap, egging on the rest of
the bus.

175

"Tenley, how could you?" Pennie whispered.

Tenley looked miserable.

"Fairy-licious, show us your propellers," a student called up to her. Other students began videoing Pennie with their phones.

Until Mr. Mingby walked up the stairs.

"Quiet down now."

No one did.

"Students, please. Quiet down now." Mr. Mingby waved his hands for emphasis. "Miss Tylwyth, Mr. Wonderbolt, new girl, find your seats."

Tenley turned to the back of the bus. Holden and Pennie slid into the first row, the last two empty seats together. But the noise level remained the same.

"Quiet!" Mr. Mingby yelled. A few of the silent kids glanced up before dropping their heads down to their phones again.

Red-faced, Mr. Mingby opened his mouth to yell when a large woman in a uniform appeared next to him.

She popped her thumb and forefinger into her mouth and whistled.

The bus fell silent.

"My name is Ms. Shareen and *this*"—she pointed to the floor—"is *my* bus. I take things *very personally* on my bus. That means no eating, no gum, no graffiti, no drinking, no littering, and no profanity. You do any of these things." She wagged her finger and pointed toward the window. "I drop you off out there. I pull my baby over and you're out. Questions?"

There were a few rumblings, but no one raised a hand.

"I got eyes right here." She pointed to her rearview mirror.

"They see it all. I can see what color lip-gloss y'all have on." A boy laughed, but Ms. Shareen's glare shut him down. "Mr. Teacher, you got anything else to say?" She turned to Mr. Mingby with her hands on her generous hips.

Mr. Mingby, looking mesmerized by her, broke his stare and nodded to the group. "Be respectful, students. We'll be off school premises so if you do something you *shouldn't*, you'll get arrested and we'll all just stand there and watch." Mr. Mingby looked back to Ms. Shareen for approval. She nodded affirmatively.

"All right then. ETA is seven-thirty, give or take. Let's get you to Adventures, Inc.!" She clapped once and squeezed into the driver's throne. Mr. Mingby sat in the single seat catty-corner from her.

Pennie felt a heaviness worse than gravity fill her chest. Tenley had exposed her identity with the video, which meant if the Fair Force deemed it necessary, they would have to erase the memory of every single person who saw it. That wouldn't go over well with the Fairships.

"Why did you tell Tenley all those weird things?" Holden asked.

"I didn't, I mean, the thing is, I was in a play. At my old school. And I was saying my lines, you know, acting them out with her."

"Oh." Holden chuckled. He stood and turned to the back of the bus. "It was a *play*, morons. She was *acting out* her lines in a *play*." Only a few kids looked like they'd heard him, but already those few kids were telling a few of the other kids.

Pennie exhaled quietly.

Holden sat again and held his phone up to her.

"What are you doing?"

"Documenting the first time I sat next to you on a bus."

Something hit Holden in the back of his head. He looked up into Ms. Shareen's rearview mirror, but she'd missed it.

"Holden, you have something in your hair," Pennie said.

"What is it?" He ripped out a chunk along with a wad of gum. When he saw what it was, he shifted around to see who'd thrown it. No one made eye contact.

"I hate it here," Holden said, turning back and throwing the wad of hair and gum on the floor before remembering Ms. Shareen and her mirror. But she'd missed this too.

"Where?" Pennie asked.

"Here. School."

"It will get better, Holden," Pennie said softly.

"Sit your butt down back there!" Ms. Shareen yelled. A boy stood frozen in the middle of the aisle.

"Lost my paperclip." The boy smirked, holding up a paperclip to prove it and then scurried back to his seat.

"If I were *that* guy, I'd probably love it here," Holden said.

"That guy?" Pennie asked. "What does he have that you don't?"

"Let's see. That guy rules the school. So, respect, for one thing. He can do whatever he wants." Holden snorted lightly. "Like that lacrosse jerk. Same thing. They were just born lucky." He glanced down at his cast. "Not like me."

"Someday, Holden, you're going to find out just how lucky you are."

Holden snorted again.

"It might not seem like it now," Pennie said. "But you're a special guy, Holden Wonderbolt. And you're going to do great things. Try to remember that."

"Would you go out with me?" he asked quietly. Then he turned to her with his cheeks flushed. "I mean like *would* you. Not would *you*?"

"Yes," Pennie said. "If I were a girl in your class, I would."

"You are a girl in my class."

The bus started to move, and quickly screeched to a stop. Mr. Mingby's paperwork flew off his lap and into the aisle. While Ms. Shareen honked at the squirrel in the middle of the road, Holden leaned over and gathered everything up for Mr. Mingby.

"Thank you, Mr. Wonderbolt."

"No problem, Mr. Mingby."

Pennie smiled proudly. And hoped Laraby was too.

Something buzzed.

"I think your dinosaur alarm just went off," Holden said.

Pennie looked at her wrist. **01:00:00**. The one-hour mark. The Fair Force were on their way.

"I love that you wear a dinosaur watch," Holden said. "What's it counting down?"

Pennie looked back at Tenley.

"How long I have left on Earth with Tenley."

"You wish." Holden laughed.

32

00:20:00
Adventures, Inc.

Forty minutes later, Ms. Shareen jerked the bus into park. "Adventures, Inc., people!" she announced, as if the gigantic, three-story neon *Adventures, Inc.* sign wasn't visible enough.

The students rushed into the aisle, including Pennie. She had twenty minutes to get Tenley as far away from everyone else as possible.

Before anyone reached the doors, Ms. Shareen whistled again.

"Children, you are going to leave my bus in an *orderly manner*. No pushin', shovin', textin'. *I* see any funny business, *you* stay on the bus. I could use a smarty pants to help me with my Sudoku." She elbowed Mr. Mingby standing next to her. "Picking up what I'm laying down, Mr. Teacher Man?"

Apparently, Mr. Mingby was. He nodded and said,

"Remember, students. We cannot be responsible for lost items such as cell phones, iPads, iPods, you-hoo's. So we suggest you leave them on the bus." He waited for Ms. Shareen to laugh but really, it was a fail of a joke, so she turned back to the students who were stepping all over each other waiting to get off.

"Back rows, you start," Ms. Shareen waved.

The students filtered out of their rows as instructed.

Ms. Shareen elbowed Mr. Mingby proudly. "And *that's* how it's done, Mr. Teacher Man."

"Call me Stan," Mr. Mingby said.

"I'll do that, Stan. And you can call me Ms. Shareen."

Outside, two boys were already tackling each other by the time everyone was finally off the bus.

"Get over here." Ms. Shareen pointed to them. "Now which one of you is better at Sudoku?"

Neither answered.

"Words with Friends?"

No answer.

Pennie tried to get Tenley's attention, but when she waved to her, the lacrosse boy mimed flapping wings at her again.

"You look smarter." Ms. Shareen pointed to the smaller of the two petrified boys.

The small boy shook his head. "I'm bad at stuff like words."

Ms. Shareen crossed her arms. "I don't like the look of them, Mr. Teacher Man. I think you'll be needin' some help with these tweens and things. Mind if I come along?"

"I was hoping you would, actually," Mr. Mingby blushed.

A girl next to Tenley put her finger down her throat and

pretended to gag.

Ms. Shareen climbed back onto the bus, peeled off her bus-driver sweater, and locked the door after she stepped out again. "Adventures Inc., let's see what you got!"

33

00:12:01
Adventures, Inc.

Pennie scanned the layout as they walked farther inside the park.

"Sit next to me on the roller coaster?" Holden asked.

Pennie nodded but looked away. She had only minutes now.

When the roller coaster came into view, most of the students broke out of their groups and sprinted toward it.

"Do we *have* to go on?" a girl asked Mr. Mingby, who looked a little green himself.

"Sure don't," he said, taking off his glasses and cleaning them with his shirt. "In fact, I'm happy to sit this one out myself." He slid his glasses back on. "Those who want to go on the ride, get in line. Those who would rather not, stay with me."

A few more students stepped forward, but Pennie didn't move. She had just spotted an area beyond the merry-go-round that looked empty.

"Aren't you coming?" Holden asked.

"I'm not really into heights." Pennie answered.

"But you said you'd sit with me."

To the left of the roller coaster was a small shed they could also hide behind. "My stomach's feeling a little funny. Is it okay if I wait for you over there?"

"I'll stay with you." Holden deflated. "There's too many jerks around here." He narrowed his eyes at a group of boys laughing at Pennie.

"Holden, please go." If he didn't leave soon, the Fair Force would have to erase his memory.

The alarm on her stopwatch went off. The ten-minute warning.

"I think your dinosaur's calling again," Holden grinned.

"You should go on. Please."

"You coming, Mr. Teacher Man?" Ms. Shareen called back from the front of the line.

"I'll sit this one out." He waved to her on his tiptoes.

Ms. Shareen stormed over, grabbed his elbow, and dragged him into the front of the line with her.

"Mingby's got more game than you, Wonderbolt!" A few boys smirked, patting him on the shoulder. "How about you and your fairy go on over to the Log Ride?" They flapped their imaginary wings and cracked each other up.

"Very funny. Why don't you losers go on it instead?" Tenley snickered, but when she pointed over to it, she froze.

Dan Ringer was standing in front of it.

"Dan!" Tenley waved. "Hey Danny, it's me, Tenley!"

"Omigod! Dan Ringer!" A group of girls squealed.

Dan nodded politely, but when he noticed Pennie, he broke out into a wide smile. "Hey there, Pennie, Holden. You guys on a field trip this early?"

"Yeah," Tenley answered, flipping her hair. "What are you doing here?"

"Community Service Work. I'm a Big Brother. I'm meeting my Little Brother here."

"Wanna come on the roller coaster with us?" Tenley asked.

"I'm not much of a heights guy," Dan said.

"Me neither." Tenley stepped out of the line. "These things make me barf."

Tenley sauntered over to Dan, who looked increasingly miserable.

Pennie's heart raced. "Hey, come back Tenley. I need to talk to you for a second. In private?"

Tenley ignored her.

"We should go save him," Holden told Pennie. "I heard he's the assistant coach next year. And he knows *my name*. I had no idea he knew my name."

A few small children and their parents, yawning and holding coffee cups, were the only people in line at the Log Ride.

Holden pressed on. "He has *power*. Power to *play* people. Come on. It's the least you could do for someone who taught you how to skateboard."

Holden started over to them. Reluctantly, Pennie followed.

Dan Ringer greeted them with a genuine smile but ignored

Tenley who tugged on his arm. "Hey. Let's all go on it!" she said. "It'll be fun!"

The waterfall was much bigger than it seemed from the roller coaster line.

Tenley snuggled closer to Dan. "Come on, Danny. It's higher than it looks. I'll go with you." She pulled him into the line with her and glanced back. "You two, come on!"

Holden shrugged at Pennie. "I'm game if you are?"

There was no way she was going to get Tenley away from Dan. The Fair Force would have to erase his memory too. "Okay, sure," Pennie said, stepping into the line with him.

A boy in front of Dan dropped his mother's hand and turned around.

Dan smiled.

The boy kept staring at him.

"Small child?" Tenley pointed to her sash. "Can you read this? I'm Tenley T. Do you think that tonight you could get your entire family to vote for me?"

The mother turned around and the boy pointed up to Dan. "Him!"

"Oh, no," Tenley said. "He's not trying to get nominated. I am. America's Next Most Inspirational Teen!" she cheered.

"How exciting," the mom said. "What is it that you do to inspire teens?"

"Nail art," Tenley answered proudly. "Building confidence one nail at a time."

"Interesting." The mother turned her son around quickly. "It's our turn, honey." They walked through the entrance.

A little girl ran up behind Pennie. "Again, again!" she cried, holding a stuffed bunny.

"Sorry, Sweets, we don't have time." The girl's father hurried after her with a squirming toddler in his arms.

"Please, Daddy?" The little girl pouted. "*Please?*"

The father shook his head.

"Go ahead of us, sir," Dan Ringer offered, stepping aside.

"Are you sure?" the father asked.

"Pleasepleasepleasepleaseplease?" the little girl begged.

"Thanks an awful lot." The father slid by the four of them. The moment the entrance gate opened, the little girl took off toward the empty log. "Wait!" The father hurried after her, shifting the toddler into his other arm.

Dan and Tenley were next. The attendant, who looked much in need of some sleep and allergy medication, eyed them suspiciously and pointed to a sign on the wall. *Limit 280 pounds.* Then he sneezed. Twice.

"Looks like I'm going to have to go with Pennie," Dan said, stepping back.

There was no arguing. Pennie was a good twenty pounds lighter. Tenley growled and yanked Holden up beside her. "Come on, Wonderbutt."

"Bolt."

Holden groaned but complied with the attendant who waved them through to the next free log.

"Keep your hands inside the log at all times," the attendant said, before sneezing again and throwing his well-used tissue into the trash.

Holden and Tenley climbed inside the log.

Pennie's wrist buzzed. She couldn't tell if Dan had noticed. **00:03:00**.

"I think I'll just watch from over there, Dan," Pennie said.

But when the attendant waved them forward, Dan hooked her elbow into his.

"I insist," he said quietly.

"Keep your hands in at all times," the attendant said, then sneezed. This time he blew into his sleeve and rubbed his eyes. "Hey! Any a-you's got a tissue by any chance?"

Both Dan and Pennie shook their heads. Pennie climbed into the log first and buckled her seatbelt. Dan climbed in after her.

The logs jerked to a start. The loudspeaker rattled off: *"The Log Ride will now begin. Please make sure your seatbelt is buckled. Keep hands and feet in at all times. Splashing may occur."*

Holden, in the log directly in front of them, turned around. He looked miserable next to Tenley. Their log began climbing the backside of the steep waterfall.

Pennie checked her watch. **00:02:00**.

Dan stared straight ahead, until a high-pitched screech made everyone look.

It was the little girl in the log ahead of Holden and Tenley. She was out of her seatbelt. "My bunny!" she cried, climbing on top of her seat. Her father reached around to grab the back of her pants while balancing the squirming toddler on his lap. "Emmie, sit down!" he yelled.

"Hey!" Holden screamed down to the attendant. "A little girl dropped her bunny. Turn off the ride!"

The attendant was nowhere to be seen.

"Someone stop the ride!" the father yelled. He twisted around desperately to keep hold of his daughter.

Holden undid his seatbelt and stood on unbalanced legs. He waved his arms down to the empty attendant stand. "Hey! Someone. Anyone! Turn off the ride!"

"Be careful, Holden," Pennie yelled up to him. Dan stayed quiet.

Pennie could see the stuffed bunny floating in the water. It was caught in the downward current heading for Tenley's side of the log. Holden saw it too.

"Tenley, grab it when it comes by."

"I'm not touching this water, gross!"

The little girl shrieked louder the farther up their log chugged away from her bunny.

"*Come on!*" Holden frowned at Tenley. "You'll be doing something *inspiring*."

"Omigod, you're right," she realized.

"Lean over and grab it," Holden coached her.

"Okay. Video it for me!" She handed him her phone.

When the bunny reached their log, Tenley leaned over, pinched one of the ears, and lifted it out of the water.

Before she sat back again, she hiked the bunny up over her shoulder. "Here, kid."

"No!" Holden yelled.

But it was too late. Tenley had thrown the bunny upstream.

The bunny sailed over the rushing falls and hit the little girl on the shoulder before bouncing off and falling into the water all over again.

The little girl went into hysterics. Her log chugged up higher.

"What's the matter with you? Why'd you do *that*?" Holden groaned. He handed her back her phone. Then he leaned over her, to get ready to swoop up the bunny again.

"Watch the sash," Tenley said. "That was a perfect throw."

Holden extended his reach. "I think I got it," he said just before tumbling into the water.

It was only a few feet deep but the current was hard to stand against. "I'm okay," Holden said, splashing to keep upright. But he didn't look like it.

Pennie turned to Dan. "Dan, can you pull him in?"

Dan shook his head.

There were bigger problems ahead now and Tenley was the only one to notice. The little girl had broken free from her father's grip and before he could get hold of her again, she toppled out.

"Help!" the father shouted, standing with the toddler. "Please, someone grab her!"

Twisting and churning, the little girl cried but her screams were muffled by the sounds of the rushing water.

"Swim, little thing!" Tenley called up to her, but the little girl was starting to sink. Holden was too far back in the water to reach her now. "Someone help her!" Tenley yelled.

The father and his toddler were looking like they might fall over themselves.

"I can't swim. Can you?" Pennie asked Dan.

"No."

Pennie's alarm went off.

00:00:30.

Dan had no reaction.

"Tenley. *You* have to get her," Holden shouted. "Grab her and pull her inside."

"My Brazilian blow-out can't get wet!"

Holden coughed out water. He was starting to submerge "You'll be on TV! There are security cameras everywhere. Go!"

Tenley considered this. "You think?"

"You'll get so many votes tonight!"

That was all Tenley needed to hear. She threw one leg over the side of the log, flipped back her hair, rearranged her short shorts, plugged her nose, and jumped in.

"Hold on, small child," she yelled, waist deep in water. "Tenley Tylwyth is coming."

But the little girl was gone.

Pennie couldn't sit by any longer. She started climbing out until Dan pushed her back to sitting. "I wouldn't do that."

A shiver went up Pennie's spine. Something was wrong with Dan.

"Where'd you go, little thing?" Tenley searched the water. "*Ow.* Hey. It's you." She pulled the little girl up by the waist.

"Emmie!" The father waved. His log was only a few meters from the crest of the waterfall now.

Emmie choked and cried.

"Don't worry, I got her!" Tenley shouted to her father. Except she was beginning to lose her footing against the current as well.

191

Holden started fighting his way up to them. "Just hang on, Tenley. I'll take her." But his next step landed him underwater again.

"Listen—thing," Tenley pleaded. "Please—stop—squirming—can't—"

Tenley turned her face upwards and looked at the sky. Pennie noticed. She knew that look.

"No, Tenley! You signed the form—"

Pennie's alarm went off. **00:00:10**

Tenley threw the little girl up as high as she could and blew out a quick breath. The gust of wind caught little Emmie and suspended her midair until Tenley blew out another breath, this one slightly more controlled. The little girl began blowing upward across the waterfall headed directly for her father's log, which was just cresting the other side now.

And in what could only be seen as a miracle, milliseconds before his log disappeared, Emmie's father caught her.

Holden started to cheer but the force with which Tenley had thrown the little girl was strong enough to keep pulling Tenley over the side of the waterfall.

"Tenley!" Holden screamed, lunging his hand out for her foot.

Just as he caught it, a huge roar, not unlike the sound of marbles getting stuck in a vacuum cleaner, covered everything like a blanket.

34

00:00:07
Adventures, Inc.

"**G**ood day, Commander."

"Your Fairship." Dan saluted the figure hovering above him.

"I apologize for being a little early. This group was very *eager* to get here."

Dan stepped out of the log and directly onto the water, which was frozen in jagged splashes. Pennie squeezed her eyes, then opened them again. Dan Ringer? Why was he talking to Fair Force?

Pennie wiggled her fingers and touched her face. Everything around her was frozen. And every*one*. Holden's frozen body stretched across the hardened waterfall with one hand grabbing Tenley's ankle. Tenley's body was halfway over the side, her long blond hair fanning out behind her and a look of sheer terror on her face. They were at least twenty meters off the ground.

"Just another day at the human zoo, I see," a snarky voice said.

Pennie recognized it.

Lady Fairship slipped off her hood and sneered down at the frozen scene of weary parents and screaming children littering the grounds of the theme park.

"Ah, there you are, Fair One PENN 1. Commander," she turned to Dan, "why don't you tell me what's going on here?"

"There was an incident. Ten seconds before your arrival, your Fairship. I believe the client used her element again."

"It was only to help a little girl!" Pennie shouted up to her.

"Silence, Fair One!" Lady Fairship ordered. "Still with the interrupting, I see."

Pennie shut her mouth. Arguing with Lady Fairship could only end badly.

"So am I to understand that we travelled all this way to complete the deletion process, only to discover that ten seconds ago the client broke the contract and once again used her element?"

"Yes, your Fairship. I will contact Headquarters to inform them that we will be transporting the client back with us for a complete erase now instead." Dan revealed his tool belt under his dark-blue hoodie.

"What? No!" Pennie yelled. "You don't understand!"

Lady Fairship dropped lower to address her. "I'm not sure what you think we don't understand. Commander DNRGR has been monitoring the attempt on your client's Right to Delete, which was about to be found successful. Your client *would have* remained here on Earth as a non-elemented human."

"But I told you—" Pennie stepped forward, tripping on a jagged splash of frozen water.

"However, after this latest development, we find ourselves right back where we started in Room Thirty-three. Your client is headed to Fair City for an Immediate Erase." Lady Fairship snapped at the Fair Force above her. "And unfortunately, you, Fair One, are to be banished."

Two Fair Force zoomed down and grabbed Pennie's shoulders.

"Your Fairship! My client had no choice. The little girl was drowning. She was going to *die*."

"I'm sad to hear it. Arrest her."

The Fair Force jerked Pennie's arms behind her.

Pennie kicked at one of them, hitting his knee. She kicked the other one in the thigh. Both of them groaned and released their grips.

Pennie felt herself lift off the ground anyway.

"Sorry, your Fairship." It was Dan. "It's the gravity. Most of the Force aren't up to speed yet." But Dan, of course, was plenty acclimated. He kept his hold on Pennie while she remained hovering a few feet off the ground.

Lady Fairship crossed her arms. "Attacking Fair Force now, Fair One? Are you hoping to get your entire family banished as well?"

"My family? No, please, Lady Fairship." The thought of her mother and siblings left to float in space for all eternity made Pennie go weak.

Lady Fairship enjoyed watching her threat take hold. "It's *one* order away."

Dan tightened his grip.

"You two," Lady Fairship ordered the recovering Fair Force. "Get the client."

"Lady Fairship," Pennie said feebly. "Could my client see her mother one last time?"

Lady Fairship rolled her eyes. "You're the most pitiful Fair One in Fair City. You were obviously too emotional for the job anyway."

Pennie felt a thud on her head. Fair Force were not allowed to use aggressive force against a Fair One, but that was in Fair City. Who knew what they could do here.

It wasn't just Pennie who was getting bombarded, though. Fair Force all around started to duck and take cover. Loud clankings were followed by painful crunching sounds while whatever it was falling through the air began hitting propellers. A few blades crunched down to a momentary halt before throwing off whatever had clogged them.

Stroons. Raining down from a wind tunnel above them.

A pair of Fair Force backed into each other with a sickening crunch of their blades. They landed hard on top of the frozen water. Another stroon hit Pennie on the shoulder. Lady Fairship pulled something out of her tool belt. A hologram wand.

The rest of the Fair Force pulled out the same device. Dan kept a tight hold on Pennie as he reached for his and pointed it at the wind tunnel.

"Fair Force! On my com—"

Before he finished, the wind tunnel broke apart into a swirl of white robes with a long red beard and a bald head on top.

Laraby.

Fair Force grabbed him quickly. Laraby raised both arms in surrender.

"Name and rank," Lady Fairship demanded.

"Fair One, LARA B3, your Fairship," he stuttered. "I'm sorry about the stroons, they flew out of my robes."

"Arrest him."

"Rule #567893 under section Z03965 in *The Rules and Regulations!*"

Lady Fairship glared at him. "What?"

"Rule #567893: *A client who risks his own life to save another life nullifies any and all elemental infractions up to said point and time.*" Laraby spoke so quickly he had to catch his breath. He sneaked a look down at Pennie, glanced back at the two Fair Force holding him, and then returned to Lady Fairship, who still had yet to respond. "Which *means,*" he continued, "that Fair One PENN 1's client no longer needs to be erased."

Lady Fairship narrowed her eyes.

"In other words," Laraby said, pointing at the waterfall. "Fair One PENN 1's client saved that little girl's life. She risked her own life to do so. Which means that using her element again was, in this case, not a crime. The client may continue on with her Right to Delete, and after her powers have been deleted, she may remain on Earth as an un-elemented human. And Fair One PENN 1 no longer needs to be banished." He paused. "Should I say it again? Or are we all good?"

Fuming, Lady Fairship propelled herself closer to the waterfall to inspect the frozen Tenley. After a quick look, she summoned Dan, who dropped Pennie back down on top of the frozen water.

"Are you sure about this, Lar?" Pennie whispered.

"Completely." Laraby nodded. Then hesitated. Then nodded again. "I'm completely sure. Oh, and I got your subtle not-so-subtle request for the hologram ad. I brought the Intel."

"No talking," one of the Fair Force warned.

Dan propelled back over to them. Lady Fairship kept her distance.

"It seems," Dan reported. "Fair One LARA B3 is correct. Rule #567893 applies. You may release him, Fair Force."

Laraby landed with a smack on top of the frozen water. He winced and gathered himself to stand.

"Thank you, Laraby." Pennie's voice shook.

"It was luck, really." He tapped on his earpiece. "I just happened to be listening to the audio version of *The Manual* right before the journey down here, and then I overheard what was going on."

"Fair Force, you may prepare the client for permanent deletion of her element upon our return to Fair City," Dan ordered.

A Fair Force holding a skullcap with various cords attached to it started toward the frozen Tenley.

"Wait, Commander!" One of the Fair Force propelled closer to Dan. "We have a problem, sir. There are seven seconds left on the clock."

Dan looked confused.

"We'll need to let those expire before our systems can begin the return transportation process."

"I see," Dan said.

Lady Fairship zoomed over. A wide smile crossed her face. "We will allow the seven seconds to pass, then. After which, we will see what we're left with."

Laraby mumbled something.

Pennie turned to him. "Seven seconds? But—"

"Exactly," Laraby agreed. "Excuse me, your Fairship, Commander. As you can see, the client is in a clear and present danger. It's highly unlikely she will survive the seven seconds."

Pennie's heart sank. If time resumed where it left off, Tenley, and maybe even Holden, would plummet over the waterfall. There would be no need for a permanent deletion. *Or* an immediate erase. The waterfall was too high.

"My client, too, is in a dangerous position," Laraby continued.

"Yes, I see that. Pity. Commander?" Lady Fairship turned to him. "What are the chances of either client surviving the fall?"

"Zero."

"Your Fairship," Laraby tried to sound casual. "If we could only turn back a little time to get both clients to safety—"

"Lovely thought. Can't be done." Lady Fairship nodded to Dan, who turned away to signal the rest of the troops. "We are not allowed to turn back time on Earth, only freeze it temporarily, as I'm sure *you,* Fair One LARA B3, are very well aware. Rule #1, section *1.* You will have seven seconds to save them."

Pennie felt her knees buckle.

"But the problem is how?" Lady Fairship continued. "You don't have your tools. And we are not authorized to lend you ours. I have an idea though." She propelled lower to Pennie. "If you were to use a Renegade Weather to help you here, to bring your clients to safety so we can proceed with the transport and deletion, we'll look the other way this time. In fact, we'll even help you contact one."

She gave Dan a silent order.

"In exchange, however, you, Fair One PENN 1, will be required to stay here on Earth. We can explain to Headquarters that you were simply overcome with despair when your client was deleted of her element. You were *so distraught*, in fact, that you stole our tools and removed your own ID chip to remain untraceable to Fair Force forevermore. Sound good?"

"You want me to remove my chip?" Pennie touched the back of her head where the chip had been implanted.

Lady Fairship hovered higher. "Do I detect some hesitation? How very peculiar. One would have expected you to jump at the chance to avoid Administration and stay here with your beloved client. Now I'm wondering if it was just her element that made you so fond of her. Her personality is rather, shall we say, self-absorbed?"

Pennie's head began to swirl. Staying here with Tenley Tylwyth for the rest of her life? Posting nail tutorials? And after Tenley was gone, what then? A Fair One could live for up to two hundred years. Two hundred years on planet Earth with no purpose. No identity. No propellers.

Laraby cleared his throat. "Excuse me, Lady Fairship, but

removing a Fair One's identity chip is against *Manual* rules."

A flash of rage crossed Lady Fairship's face. "Fortunately, there are still a few top-secret privileges the Original Eights possess, Fair One." She turned to Pennie. "We'll need your answer rather immediately, I'm afraid."

Pennie looked over at Tenley. Dan was right; there was no chance that she'd survive the fall. In the next seven seconds, Tenley would be dead.

"Holden might make it," Pennie said quietly.

Pennie felt a punch in her gut for Mrs. Tylwyth. If Tenley had been erased, all memories of her would have been erased as well. But not this way. This way, Mrs. Tylwyth was going to lose her child in a tragic accident. And be heartbroken forever.

She couldn't let that happen.

"Call in the Renegade Weathers. I'll stay."

"No!" Laraby yelled.

"Yes," Pennie nodded sadly.

Lady Fairship propelled higher and addressed her troops. "Fair One LARA B3 will need to have all memory of this incident stripped. Deliver him to City Hall upon our return. And you," she pointed to a small petrified Fair Force. "You will remove PENN 1's ID Chip and make sure it gets scrambled. Transport will be sent for you immediately following."

The petrified Fair Force dipped his head. "Yes, Lady Fairship."

Two Fair Force dropped down to retrieve Laraby.

"Please, Pennie, make sure the Renegade Weathers catch my client too," he said.

Pennie's eyes started to tear.

"Prepare to evacuate," Lady Fairship ordered. "Present time will resume in sixty seconds."

"Wait! The Renegade Weathers," Pennie panicked. "You haven't called them in yet!"

Lady Fairship snickered before pulling her hood up. Above her, a white vortex was falling through the sky.

"Lady Fairship, the Weathers! You said you'd call them!" Laraby screamed.

Lady Fairship activated her propellers, shot up toward the vortex, and disappeared inside it.

"She lied to us," Laraby yelled down to Pennie. "She's going to let them die."

"What do we do?"

"Family is always there to catch you when you fall!" Laraby cried out.

The entire fleet of Fair Force, save the one waiting with Pennie, began propelling up into the whirling vortex, which was hovering now.

"Family is always there to catch you when you fall!" Laraby shrieked again.

Pennie felt a crack under her. She jumped off the water. "Time is about to restart!"

"Full strength!" a Fair Force yelled. "Commander, we need full strength."

Something was wrong. Fair Force had begun slipping out of the vortex. Fierce winds were bombarding it now and it wasn't just the water that was cracking, but the ground. Big chunks of land were pulling apart and the Log Ride had begun to shake.

Pennie jumped off another crack just in time.

"More power!" Dan yelled above her.

Instead of lifting up farther, the whirling vortex was sucked sideways into a gigantic swirling tornado.

Bodies spewed out of the tornado and crashed onto the ground. One of them was Lady Fairship. Her hood had blown off and her sleeve was torn. The same crystal eight could be seen hanging around her neck. Laraby noticed it just before Lady Fairship produced a jetpack from her tool belt, strapped it on, and shot upwards again.

"Jet packs!" Dan ordered the rest of the Fair Force, some of whom were still spewing out of the tornado. "Evacuate now! Everyone!"

The Fair Force who had been assigned to stay behind with Pennie pulled out his jet pack and shot upward along with the rest of the Fair Force.

Streams of white lines were all that remained.

Water gurgled down the log ride. Time had resumed.

"Family is always there to catch you when you fall!"

Pennie turned to find Laraby sprawled out on the ground next to her. "Laraby! Are you okay?"

There was no time to answer.

A scream pierced the air.

High above them, Tenley's arms were flailing as Holden gripped her ankle.

They were both falling over the side of the Log Ride.

Just before impact, blackness absorbed all of them.

35

Mother Nature's Garden

Tenley landed on a pile of leaves.

"This is the worst field trip *ever*." She spit a leaf out of her mouth and straightened her sash. "Where's that little kid with the bunny? Did I get on TV?"

Tenley's hair was tangled with angry-looking branches and swipes of dirt crisscrossed her face. When she stood, her soaking wet short shorts were ripped clear up one side. "Not my short shorts."

Holden had landed a few feet away. He was in the same basic shape as Tenley: a ripped sleeve hung down one shoulder and his face was covered in smudges. He inspected his cast, but it looked intact. "That was freaky."

"Ya *think*? One second we're on the Log Ride and I'm hurling that small child up to its father, and the next second I'm falling through the air and landing here, in this"—she glanced at the trees and bushes—"weird-looking forest, with *you*. Dan? Mr. Ming-*bay*! Where are you?"

Holden stood. "This place is kind of weird."

"It looks worse than *our* garden."

For as far as they could see the foliage was dark. Tree trunks were bent over and broken. The trees that were still standing had plenty of leaves but all of them were black. The ground was covered in broken branches.

"Maybe this is the new theme park. The VR one," Holden said.

"Very Rich?" Tenley crinkled up her nose.

"Virtual Reality."

"Well, they obviously ran out of money before they finished it."

"Maybe it's like a virtual reality survivor game. We have to find our way out of this post-apocalyptic forest."

"Omigod. Do you see cameras anywhere?" Tenley broke out into a power smile.

Holden leapt over a fallen trunk. "No."

Tenley dropped her smile. "Those shows are so fake anyway. Like anyone could really survive wearing *one* bikini for an entire *month*." She checked on her sash. "We gotta get going. I have to find out if a video of me saving that small child can get uploaded to my YouTube, like *right now*."

The ground snapped. Everywhere Holden stepped, there were dry, cracking twigs. "I just remember falling through the air and then nothing."

"Ow." Tenley's hair caught in a branch. She pulled it out and noticed the black grime on her Ugg boots. "My Uggs! That's it. I'm outta here. There's gotta be an exit." She hurried off.

Holden gathered a handful of leaves. "I've never seen these kinds of leaves before," he muttered to himself.

"Whoa!" Tenley screeched. "This is ba-*nanas*."

Holden dropped the leaves and hurried over to where she was standing. "Are those daisies?"

"Who plants black and white flowers? Isn't that, like, so eighties or something?"

"*No one* plants black and white flowers. We're in a theme park."

"We had better set designs in third grade."

Holden plucked a daisy. "It's strange though, these are real. Not plastic or dried up or dead or anything. Just colorless. It's like," he twisted the stem around in his fingers, "the color has been drained out of it."

Tenley pulled a face. "Whatever. They're ugly."

"I think they're kind of cool." Holden lowered his voice and glanced around. "Hey. You think we're the only ones here?"

Tenley put a hand on his shoulder. "I'm flattered, Wonderbread."

"Bolt."

"But I'm interested in Dan." She dropped her arm. "Well, he's interested in *me*. I'm pretty sure."

"You're right. There's gotta be an exit somewhere." Holden walked away.

"Wait! Don't leave me here!" Tenley hurried after him.

After a few more steps, Holden stopped. "Look at that." He

squatted down to a flat stone with writing across it. "It's in Latin or something. Can you read it?"

"Sorry, I can't read weird."

"I wish I had my phone. I could translate it." Holden stood, turned away, and tripped. This time he landed on his cast. He clenched his jaw and sat up. A glass bottle rolled under his foot. "*Tornado*?"

"What?"

"That's what is says on the label."

Something was swirling around inside of it.

"I think there's a bug in there."

"Ew."

"Wait—" When he looked closer, he saw a tiny tornado howling inside. "That is *so cool*. There's a mini tornado in there."

Tenley grabbed it. "Let me see."

While she studied the bottle, something else caught Holden's eye. A shiny object under a pile of twigs.

"Wait a minute." He pulled it out. "This is Pennie's." It was her crystal eight. "Pen-*nie*?" he shouted. "Pennie? I know you're here. Can you hear me?"

When no answer came, he slipped the crystal eight into his pocket. "At least we know she's here, too."

"Listen, Wondernut," Tenley said, dropping the bottle on the ground. "Before you get all crush-gone-bad, I think I should tell you that Pennie's planning on leaving soon."

"She is?"

Tenley nodded. "I don't know where. I just know she's leaving."

"Well, I bet you're going to miss her then." With that, he walked on, snapping more twigs underfoot.

"I'm calling my mom." Tenley followed after him.

"How? You left your phone in the bus. You going to bounce a satellite connection off your earring?"

Tenley reached up to her faux diamond studs, then smirked. "Unless we use your braces?"

Holden dropped his head back and pulled his lips apart. "Like this?"

Tenley tried not to giggle. She covered her mouth to hide it, but Holden had seen it anyway. "By the way," he said. "That was a good job saving that little kid. How did you do that?"

Tenley looked around to make sure no one was listening. "It's this weird thing I can do. I sort of think that I want the wind to blow, and then it does."

Holden stared at her. "That's impossible."

"You know what, forget it. I have no idea how I did it. Lucky throw, I guess."

A shuffling in the brush made them freeze.

"It's creepy in here."

"Let's go this way." Holden started over to a row of trees. "Do you see how these are sticking up the wrong way?" He pointed. "These are the roots."

"So what. They're dying. That's what happens in LA. Things *die*."

He studied the roots a little closer.

"Hold it," Tenley blurted out. "Maybe we're on a movie set, like *Avatar Twelve* or something. Omigod. This could be my first acting job."

"I just told you, these are all *real*."

"So was the forest in *Avatar*. Duh. When you put the *glasses on*?"

Holden turned around in a circle. "Do you remember anything else? Like how we got here from the Log Ride?"

"I remember throwing that kid and thinking I was going to fall over the side of the waterfall. And then, I guess I did."

Holden stomped on a pile of leaves. "That's all I remember, too."

They walked around for a little longer until a field of sunflowers sprawled out before them. Gray sunflowers.

"This place is just legit sad," Tenley sighed.

Another rustling in the branches shook them. Tenley backed up behind a tree.

"Who's there?" Holden asked.

When nothing answered, Holden stepped closer to the sunflowers. They were seeping with something. He touched the yellowish green liquid dripping off the petals.

"Tenley, you gotta see this. It's the *color* dripping of these leaves." Something buzzed by him. He swatted at it. "Get outta here."

The buzzing circled him. Holden kept swatting at it but the buzzing grew louder. And faster. A small breeze picked up around him and his hair started to ruffle.

For a split second, he felt his high-tops lift off the ground. He must have imagined it. The buzzing grew even louder and this time his high-tops definitely lifted off the ground. And stayed there.

Holden was floating.

"No way!" He wobbled before widening his stance and rebalancing himself. "*Air surfing*. Tenley! I think I found the ride. It's *awesome!*"

He lifted higher. Before he could call out Tenley's name again, he started moving toward the sunflowers. *Over* the sunflowers, actually. He was floating across the field.

When he reached the other side, the buzzing slowed and he hovered to a stop. "That was so cool."

He tried jumping off the invisible ride but was immediately lifted higher. The buzzing sound sped up and the invisible force took a sharp right. He dipped under branches, barely missing tree trunks.

"Hey game guy!" he yelled. "Can we maybe turn this down a little?"

Instead, he sped up directly toward a thick gnarled tree trunk. Moving too fast to jump off, he tucked his head and prepared to crash. Just before impact, he felt his body swerve right and around the trunk.

Holden looked back at the trunk he'd barely missed. He hadn't noticed how high he was getting but now he was swerving up and over treetops.

His stomach curled. He was going to throw up.

He closed his eyes. "Get me off of this thing!"

This time someone must have heard him. The noise quieted and he began gliding over treetops, up and down and around in soft circles. He caught his breath and rebalanced himself, just before the invisible force pulled out from under him like a rug.

He plummeted downwards, with arms and legs flailing.

Before hitting the ground, his feet collided against something midair. He fell flat on his butt. He looked down. He was seventy meters off the ground, sitting on nothing.

36

Mother Nature's Garden

Only a few seconds passed before Tenley dropped next to Holden.

She opened her mouth to speak, but it seemed the air had been knocked out of her.

"Tenley?"

She shook her head.

"Can you breathe?"

"That," she managed, "was awful."

"Don't look down."

But she did. And screamed.

She buried her head into her knees. Holden patted the space around him. "It's a web. Like a giant invisible web."

"Gross!" She tried to scoot toward one of the two trunks they had landed in between, but her foot was stuck. She yanked on it, which only made things worse.

"Don't move," Holden warned.

"That buzz. I thought it was bees. I'm allergic to them." She shivered. "I was just standing there when something started lifting me off the ground. And even when I tried to jump off, it kept getting higher. And then it just took off—"

"And started swerving around trees?"

"And then everything—"

"Stopped."

"And I landed here."

"Same thing happened to me."

Tenley's voice cracked. "I really want to go home."

Holden felt bad for her. She hadn't even checked on her sash, which had another tear across the shoulder now. She looked truly terrible.

"Can anyone hear us?" He tried to stand but a foot slipped through, trapping him with one leg hanging down. Biting his lip, he put his weight on his broken arm and pulled his leg back up through the sticky web.

"Game Master!" he shouted. "Not cool anymore."

"*Park per-son!*" Tenley yelled.

Something screeched into what sounded like a rusty start.

"Did you hear that?" Tenley asked.

Above them, a gigantic pink petal, the size of a hula-hoop, was creaking downwards. Halfway to them, it jerked to a stop. Then it started again. Just as it looked like it was going to land directly on top of Tenley, the petal jerked violently, swung to the right and then to the left, and finally slammed against the tree trunk across from them, nestling itself inside a branch.

"Snail secretions!" a voice from inside yelled. "Need a filter change!"

"Yeah. Um, hello?" Holden ventured.

The same voice fell into a coughing fit.

"Lame-alarm," Tenley whispered, rolling her eyes.

The petal shifted around until an antique-looking woman, four feet tall at most and wearing a wilted crown of purple flowers and dead branches, popped up.

"You're so old," Tenley said.

"Tenley," Holden warned, except she was right. The woman's face looked like it had been sketched in with pencil and her faded red hair was piled high under the wilting crown.

The old woman squinted back and forth at both of them. "Fair One or sipLip?" she asked in a raspy voice, pointing a crooked finger.

"Ah—" Holden hesitated.

"Wait. Did you say Fair One?" Tenley asked.

"Which one are you?" the old woman demanded.

"I'm a kid?" Holden answered.

"And you?" She pointed to Tenley.

"A more popular kid?"

The old woman considered them. "Humans. How did you get into my gardens?"

"Yeah, about that," Holden said. "We don't know. We were on the Log Ride in another part of the park, and she was about to fall over the edge," he nodded to Tenley, "the next thing we knew we landed in here instead. Somewhere down there, to be specific." He pointed through the trees.

The old woman narrowed her eyes. "What do you seek?"

"A lemonade?" Holden smiled. "I'm dying."

"How convenient," the old woman said.

Tenley frowned. "I don't want some stupid lemonade. I got my hair ripped out and my Uggs muddy. I just want to get back to our bus and wait for this whole thing to be over. I have a big night tonight." She checked on her sash and noticed the new gash in it. "No!" she cried.

The old woman shouted up to the sky. "Weathers!"

Two things happened next. First, a miniature tornado appeared out of nowhere and spun over to the old woman's shoulder where it hovered. Then a small black cloud blew in and stopped over the other shoulder, where it, too, hovered.

"How did you do that?" Tenley asked.

"Prepare to engage," the old woman ordered, plucking a wilted blade of grass from her crown and bringing it to her lips. Instead of blowing a whistle, the noise that fell out of her mouth was more like a tire going flat. "Honestly," the old woman groaned, throwing the grass down and feeling around in her crown for another blade. She plucked out a perkier one and the whistle that followed was loud enough to blow back the leaves of every tree inside the very strange forest.

Holden and Tenley slapped their hands over their ears and eyeballed each other until the old woman dropped her hands. Everything was quiet for a moment before the loud buzzing began.

"Not *again*," Tenley groaned.

But this time they could *see* the sound.

Bees.

Thousands of them began circling Holden and Tenley.

"I'm allergic!" Tenley dropped into Holden and buried her face in his shoulder. "Get them away!"

The old woman watched the swarm pick up, growing dense enough to form a solid black line around them.

She clapped her hands and ordered, "Commence!" The miniature tornado and small black cloud zoomed away. The bees stopped circling. After a beat, they started dive-bombing them. Holden covered Tenley's body as best he could and waited for the pain …

That didn't come.

The swarming sound changed into staccato spurts of angry buzzing.

Holden lifted his head. The bees were still diving straight for them but just as they were about to make contact, they bounced away. "Tenley!" Holden shook her. "They can't get to us. Look."

Tenley peeked an eye out.

"It's like there's a bubble around us or something."

The old woman had noticed this, too. She clapped again. A second army of swirling bees merged with the first. This time when the bees attacked, they could see the bubble around them wobble. "What is happening?" Tenley cried.

Black dots were piling up on the ground beneath them. The old woman watched expressionless until eventually the last of the swarm dropped away.

The forest fell silent.

"This is like a little *too* real," Holden whispered. "Even for VR."

The old woman pulled a twig out of her crown this time. "Arachnids!" she yelled, waving it.

Nothing happened. Tenley loosened her grip on Holden until small movements below caught her eye. "What are those?" Tenley whimpered. Black dots were crawling out from under the dirt.

"Those look like—"

The dots scurried over the pile of bees and clambered up the tree trunks.

"Spiders!" Holden yelled.

Tenley dived back under his arm. He tried to scoot both of them closer to the center of the web, but his arm slipped through, followed by his shoulders and head.

Tenley got to her knees and yanked him up.

They huddled together as the spiders raced up the trunks. When the first of the spiders were directly across from them on either side, Holden shook Tenley. "They can't get to us, either."

Tenley opened one eye. The spiders were crawling up and over themselves on the tree trunks. "If those things come any closer, I swear I'll jump."

Holden looked back at the old woman. "She's just standing there, watching," he whispered. "Um. Excuse me, ma'am? We didn't get any instructions, so we don't really know how this is supposed to end?"

"I'm jumping!" Tenley screamed, trying to stand.

"Wait, why?"

But there was no need for an answer. Holden could see for himself. The spiders had changed direction and were now crawling across the web, headed straight for them.

"Please, ma'am! Can you stop these spiders?" Holden asked.

The old woman's lips curled in response.

The army of spiders spread out across the net, surrounding them.

"Okay, this is bad." Holden stood up next to Tenley.

The spiders were closing in on them.

Two meters away from their feet, the spiders stopped short and started climbing upward instead, outlining the same bubble.

"I said attack, arachnids! Attack!" The old woman waved her twig.

Holden and Tenley watched the spiders crawl up and over them on either side. Their underbellies and hairy legs glistened. When the spiders met in the middle, they scuttled over themselves and continued downward again. A black line of spiders formed around them in a circle. Those that lost their grip fell to the ground and scurried up the trunks again.

The old woman shook with anger. She threw a leg over the side of the petal and stepped out. Tenley cringed when she saw what she was wearing: a shiny purple jumpsuit.

"Totally awesome special effects." Holden collected himself. "I think it's time we get back to our bus, though."

"You are *not* human."

Holden shook his head, confused. "Okay? Um. That's what it says on my birth certificate."

"Neither Fair Ones nor *humans* can defend themselves against me. Or my Weathers. Or *any* of my armies."

Tenley blinked at her. "How do *you* know about Fair Ones? Did you see the YouTube? Cuz I'm really sorry about that."

"Enough." The old woman wasn't in the mood for answering questions. She reached into her crown and pulled out an arrow, then reached in again and produced a bow. She lined the arrow up and shot it directly at Holden. It bounced off. More spiders fell to the ground. Infuriated, the old woman pressed on, shooting arrow after arrow at the bubble until all but a few spiders remained.

"You're *insane!*" Tenley yelled.

The old woman threw down the bow, exasperated. "Who brought you here?"

"Mr. *Mingby!*"

"Which kind is this?"

"Nerdy," Tenley answered.

Holden shrugged. "He's not that bad. He just doesn't have a clue."

"So this Mr. *Mingby* sent you here to find a clue? I tell *no one* of my plans. Tell him I said this: Mother Nature *always* wins. *That* is the clue."

Holden and Tenley exchanged looks.

"Trees!" the old woman summoned.

The trees around them shook. Tenley and Holden grabbed onto each other, swaying violently in the web.

"One of you has disobeyed me!" Mother Nature clapped her hands.

Lightning hit a smaller tree that exploded in the distance.

"One of you has opened your portal to these spies. When I find you, you will be struck down!" Her voice echoed throughout the forest.

She pulled another item from her crown. This time it was a clear crystal pyramid. For a moment, it looked like she might throw it at Tenley. Instead, she tucked it inside the crook of the branch, moving it just so until it reflected a white-hot ray of light directly onto the edge of the web. She stepped back into her petal.

"Weathers!" she called out. "We go!" The miniature tornado and small black cloud reappeared over her shoulders.

"Wait," Holden said, his voice constricting. "We're going to miss our bus. You can't leave us like this."

Actually, she could. Holden and Tenley watched the miniature tornado swoop down and kamikaze the pink petal, knocking it out of its niche in the tree. Next, the cloud slipped under and floated it upward. The petal jerked and banged its way back up through the leaves again.

It only took a few more seconds for the first bit of web to start melting.

37

Mother Nature's Gardens

Pennie pulled herself up from the ground and sat on a fallen tree trunk. "Laraby. Where are we? What happened?"

"I can't be sure," Laraby answered, brushing himself off and standing. He had a smear of dirt on his face and a few rips in his robes. "But I think we might be in one of her gardens."

"*Her*? You mean, *her* her?" Pennie looked around. "We're in Mother Nature's *garden*?"

"I believe so."

"What about Tenley and Holden? Do you think there's any chance they could have survived that fall?"

There was a loud explosion in the distance.

"What was that?" Pennie asked.

"Came from over there, I think." Laraby pointed.

Pennie stood. "How can we be in her gardens? Nobody

gets into her gardens. Her Weathers protect the borders. It's an impenetrable seal."

Laraby kicked at something on the ground. "Not if that impenetrable seal cracks open during a tornado attack at a theme park."

Laraby picked up a bottle and peered into it. A miniature tornado was howling inside. "I'd be willing to bet a tool or two that this was what happened up there." He held the bottle out and pointed at the label: *Tornado*.

"So that was Mother Nature attacking the Fair Force?"

"Maybe. Or it could have been just another one of her random attacks and we all got caught in it. She has hundreds of thousands of natural disasters bottled up, ready to launch."

"She keeps them lying around in her garden?" Pennie searched the ground around her feet.

"Nobody knows where she keeps them. Not even the Original Eights. If they knew where to find them, they would have been destroyed by now."

Laraby slipped the bottle into his robes and started walking again, navigating tree trunks and branches.

"These natural disasters get stronger the longer they're bottled up. I'm not even sure the Fair Force could have escaped that tornado without Lady Fairship."

Pennie hurried after him. "Lady Fairship? But *all* of the Fair Force had jetpacks."

"It was her crystal eight that saved their vortex from being blown apart. I saw it around her neck before she took off."

Pennie stopped dead in her tracks. The crystal eight. She slid her hand under Tenley's T-shirt. And felt nothing.

"Oh no."

Laraby turned around. "What is it?"

Pennie hurried back to where they had landed and kicked through a pile of leaves. "I had one, too. It was Tinktoria's. She dropped it in Command Center."

Laraby looked doubtful. "If Tinktoria had one, it means she's an Original Eight and an O-Eight never lets their crystal out of their possession. *Ever.*"

"They do if they *drop* it. I told you, Laraby, it happened during the attack."

Laraby considered this. "I think we would have heard about it. A crystal eight gone missing? That's *huge*, worthy of a City Hall announcement."

"All I know is Tink had *two* crystal eights around her neck. I saw them. She took one off to open the travel box. I bet that's the one I found." Pennie looked through more dark brush. "What else do they do besides unlock travel boxes and let things walk through walls?"

Laraby lowered his voice. "They hold undiluted, extremely potent USE. A crystal eight has been known to turn back time."

Pennie rolled a stone over onto its side. "That's against the law, even for Fair Force."

Something rustled behind a tree.

"Who's there?" Laraby stopped.

"Howdy-do!" Gavron waved. "Surprised to see me again so soon, Fairly One? Bet you were surprised to see the old bro here too, huh?"

Pennie turned to Laraby. "*This* is how you got to Earth. *Gavron*?"

Laraby nodded reluctantly.

"I mean, was that *awesome* or what? Clogging all the FF's propellers? *Not* part of the plan, b-t-dub." Gavron winked at Pennie. "I only gave my collection of stroons to my bro here as an added layer of protection for the Intel he was bringing you. Those things get scrambled crossing atmospheres unless you have some metal around them to bounce off the incoming signals. Discovered that little tidbitty myself on another top secret mission to the big E. Sorry." He held up his dirty palm. "Don't ask. Classified. Can't talk about it."

"It was a smart plan. Gavron's right," Laraby agreed. "We left Fair City right after your *conversation* with Holden about holograms."

"I think he's got a small crush on you," Gavron whispered to Pennie.

Laraby shot him a look before turning back to Pennie. "I had the Intel and the hologram ad ready but I forgot about the scrambling."

Gavron put his arm around Laraby's shoulders and winked at Pennie. "Just between you and me and him and—" He glanced around the decrepit garden and shrugged. "We weren't sure we were even going to make it. Were we, boys? It was a rough trip."

Cheers erupted from the tall gray grass behind them. The sipLips stood and waved before teetering over and disappearing again.

"Tenley and Holden," Pennie said quietly. "They didn't, I

mean, they probably—they didn't look good."

"They didn't *feel* good either. Slimy things." Gavron shuddered, wiping his hands on his robes.

Pennie blinked at him. "*Feel* good? What do you mean *feel* good?"

Laraby wiggled out from under Gavron's arm. "Gavron, are you saying family *was* there to catch them when they fell?"

"You know it, bro." Gavron high-fived him.

"Wait, *what*?" Pennie asked.

"We caught 'em." Gavron smiled his gray teeth at her.

"*Both* of them?" She could almost hug Gavron. *Almost.* "You caught both of them?"

"Well ... it was a joint effort, right, boys?"

The sipLips popped up again, drooling and waving.

Pennie looked at Laraby. "Is this true?"

"They would have no reason to lie about this, especially because if they did, the consequences would be an all-time high." Laraby glared at his brother.

Gavron threw his arms up. "Hold onto your head mobiles, Fairly Ones. It's all true."

Pennie spun around. "So where are they?"

"I dunno" Gavron shrugged. "Hey, boys, where *did* you put those slimy clients?"

The sipLips started miming their rescue, flapping their arms and snatching at the air. They continued flapping with one arm while they held something large in the other, until it looked like that something was slipping out of their hold. And then the something did slip out of their hold—you could tell by how they smashed their palms onto their foreheads, looking worried and searching the ground below.

"They dropped 'em," Gavron translated.

Pennie gasped.

"*Dropped* them, where?" Laraby asked.

Gavron wiped some drool off his chin. "Couldn't tell ya."

"*Where*, Gavron?"

Annoyed, Gavron turned back to his boys. The sipLips mimicked falling through something and landing hard on the ground. "Here," Gavron interpreted. "They fell somewhere in here, too."

Pennie stormed over and grabbed Gavron's robes. "Are they alive?"

"Idk, Fairly One. Our job was to catch them if they fell, pull them out if they drowned, lift them up if they sank. Your overall rescue operation protocol."

Pennie released him. "How did you know they were even in danger?"

"He told us." Gavron pointed to Laraby.

"You could say it was an educated guess; we *are* talking about you and your client. Now, if what Gavron is saying is true—"

"Which it is," Gavron huffed.

"It means Tenley and Holden might have survived."

Pennie turned away. "Tenley! Holden!"

"Quiet!" Laraby warned. "The last thing we want is for you-know-who to find *us* before we find *them*."

"And who would we be talking about exactly?" Gavron inquired.

"Mother Nature," Pennie answered.

Gavron exploded, suddenly trying to catch his breath. "Are you telling me we fell into her *gardens*? But that's *underground*. I can't breathe, I can't *breathe*."

"Knock it off." Laraby punched him in the shoulder. "You were breathing just fine a second ago. Obviously her gardens have their own atmosphere."

"Doesn't look like it's working too well." Gavron frowned and glanced around.

"That's because Mother Nature's gardens are but a microcosm of her bigger planet," Laraby explained.

"I knew that. Everyone knows that." Gavron cleared his throat and kicked at the ground.

"I don't," Pennie admitted.

Trying his best to be patient, although it *was* in the Manual, Laraby said, "The state of the Earth is directly reflected here in the state of these gardens. In other words, as the Earth becomes more polluted, so do these gardens. It's no wonder she wants to destroy humans."

"*Right*?" Gavron agreed.

A high-pitched yell echoed through the forest.

"Over there," Laraby pointed.

The faster they walked, the thicker and blacker the forest became and the harder it was to navigate. A few times, Laraby tripped over his robes, catching himself just before hitting the ground.

Gavron spotted them first. "There," he said, pointing up.

Seventy meters high, in between a set of trees, two figures were dangling in midair.

Pennie started to run toward them but Gavron grabbed her. "Don't."

"He's right," Laraby said.

"How are they staying there, in the air like that?"

"Webs. She hangs uninvited guests in them," Gavron whispered.

"How do you know that, Gavron?" Pennie asked.

"Let's just say not all of Mama N's Weathers are loyal to her. And me and my boys, we might hang out with few of those Renegade-types."

"Your *boys*." Laraby grabbed Gavron's shoulder. "That's it. We'll send *your boys* in to get them."

Gavron pursed his lips. "It'll cost you."

"What do I have left to give you?"

"Too true." Gavron smirked, lifting his battered robes to expose Laraby's impressive tool belt wrapped around his under-bloomers.

"You gave him your *tools*?" Pennie frowned at Laraby.

"Family might be there to catch you when you fall, but it'll cost you." Gavron dropped his robes and stepped back. "Which reminds me, this thing's a dud." He threw the garage-door opener at Pennie.

Above them, Tenley let out another shriek. Her leg had fallen through the net.

"She's falling!" Pennie panicked.

"Technically, it looks like the net is disintegrating," Laraby corrected her. "Gavron, how long do you think they have?"

"Not long."

Another scream. Holden's arm was hanging below his torso now.

"Not long at all," Gavron repeated.

"Your sipLips are the only ones quick enough and small enough to get through those branches. They're our only chance," Laraby said.

Gavron scrunched up his nose. "Okay, but like I said, I don't work for free. It sets up a bad precedent. Happened to my friend Dromo. Now he's got no respect. Can't even—"

Laraby grabbed Gavron's collar and yanked him close. "If you don't send in your boys right now—" He whispered something into his ear. Gavron's eyes went wide. He turned back to make sure the other sipLips hadn't heard.

"Videos *and* photos," Laraby added.

"You wouldn't do that," Gavron challenged him. "Those are private family moments."

Before Laraby could argue, more screams came from the trees. Tenley's arm had fallen through. Holden fought to get to her, but the more he moved, the faster the web disintegrated.

Laraby turned back to Gavron. "You have three seconds."

"Please, Gavron," Pennie begged. "They can't hold on much longer."

Gavron looked back to the sipLips before turning to Laraby again. "Fine. But you owe me." He snapped his fingers. "Go get them," he ordered the sipLips. "And make sure you wash your hands afterwards."

The sipLips activated their sorry-looking propellers and zoomed away.

229

Pennie turned to Laraby. "What did you say to him?"

"I have some videos that, let's just say, he wouldn't want to go public. Think underwear and cowboy boots."

Overhead, the sipLips popped out of the leaves and flew toward the net.

The empty net.

Tenley let out a blood-curdling scream—but not at the sipLips above them, at the ground rushing toward her below.

From Pennie and Laraby's point of view, it was impossible to know if the sipLips would reach them in time.

38

Mother Nature's Garden

"Let go of me, you freak!" Tenley screamed.

"*No!*" Pennie and Laraby yelled up to the sipLips. "Don't let go."

"Put 'em down right here, boys." Gavron directed them toward a broken tree trunk. "Nice and easy now."

The sipLips dropped Tenley and Holden with a thump and zoomed off.

"Ow!" Tenley said. "But, thank you. Thank you so much, weird things."

"Pennie!" Holden brightened. "What were those things? They had propellers."

"I'm so happy you're both okay!" Pennie turned to Laraby. "This is Laraby. He can explain everything."

"Um, I'm sorry. What are you even *wearing*?" Tenley asked.

"Uniform," Pennie answered, nodding to Laraby's torn-up robes. "He works here, so that's what he wears."

Laraby stood transfixed by Holden. Pennie elbowed him. *"Laraby."* She recognized that look. It was the same one she'd had when she'd first seen Tenley in person.

Holden's face folded. "Wait a minute. How do you know him, Pennie? I thought you'd never been to Adventures, Inc. before."

"Right, no," Pennie stalled. "We're friends."

"You have a lot of old friends."

"Where's Dan?" Tenley straightened up. "Did he see me save that little kid?"

"I think he did," Pennie told her. "He had to go."

"Wait a minute." Tenley narrowed her eyes. "Why didn't you guys have to go on that, that"—she looked to Holden for help—"whatcha call it. Stupid virtual reality invisible thing that dumped us onto that invisible net thing, where we almost *died?"*

"The visual effects were epic," Holden smiled weakly. "Except it really seemed like that lady was trying to hurt us."

This shook Laraby out of his trance. "Lady?"

"More like a witch," Tenley groaned.

"What did she look like?"

"Really old," Holden said.

"Anything else you noticed about her?"

"Uh, yeah. She's missing her heart." Tenley shivered. "She applied the crazy and just stood there while a swarm of bees attacked us and then like a million spiders crawled around us.

232

She didn't even care, she just stepped back into her lame petal and left."

"That's her," Laraby mumbled to Pennie.

"Who?" Holden asked.

"Someone else who works here," Pennie answered.

Tenley slapped her hands on her hips. "I could sue for, like, a thousand reasons. No seatbelts, for one thing. My Uggs are ruined. And we never even signed a *waiver*."

"It wasn't that bad, parts of it were pretty awesome. Like that air surfing. And those little propeller guys." Holden looked at Pennie. "I'll go on it again with you, if you want."

"I think we should get back to the bus." Pennie glanced at Laraby.

"I agree. Let's go," Tenley said.

"Pennie. We might want to look a little harder for that *thing* before we go," Laraby nudged her. "That *thing* you lost?"

"The thing I lost," Pennie reacted. "You're right. We should find it."

"Which reminds me," Holden said. "I found your necklace." He pulled it out of his pocket.

Laraby's eyes bugged. "Yes, very good. That's what she lost."

Holden handed it to Pennie.

"Thanks Holden. Where'd you—"

Something slurped.

"How about we all FaceTime later?" Tenley suggested. "This place gives me the creeps."

"Good idea," Laraby said. "Pennie, come with me. Let's look for the exit this way."

233

The two stepped away. Pennie slipped him the crystal.

Holden and Tenley followed, but stopped when they heard leaves crunching behind them.

"Howdy-do," Gavron slurped.

Tenley backed away. "Why does *no one* wash their clothes around here?"

Pennie and Laraby spun around.

"Couldn't help but overhear the gravity-groper mention a necklace. You still owe me for that broken wall opener. Mind if I take a look at it, Fair One?"

"Don't even *think* about it," Laraby warned.

"Jam your hype, bro. I was talking to the *other* Fair One."

"I don't have a necklace." Pennie held her hands up to prove it.

"Yes you do. The one with the infinity sign. I just gave it to you," Holden reminded her. "Why is everyone calling each other Fair Ones, anyway? What is that?"

"Didn't you watch the remix, Wonderall? It's like a fairy, but with tools. That's what Pennie told me."

"You told her?" Laraby turned to Pennie.

"Yup, she told me everything," Tenley answered.

Laraby threw his hands up. "Okay, now we have a serious problem."

"Aww. You took my advice, Fairly One," Gavron said proudly. "Are we in love?"

"You told your client about us because *he* told you to?" Laraby pointed at Gavron.

Holden groaned. "What is going on here? Why am I the only

one who doesn't know what any of you are talking about?"

Pennie turned to him. "Holden, what Tenley just said is true."

Holden crossed his arms. "You said it was a play, you were rehearsing your lines for a play."

Pennie looked down. "I'm sorry."

"Wait. So, you're saying you're a *fairy*?"

"*Fair One*," Tenley and Pennie said together.

Laraby groaned. "You're lucky Fair Force can't monitor us in here, Pennie, because you've just committed serious crimes. *Serious* crimes."

"I had to tell her, Lar. Nothing else was working."

"Well, now we're going to have to erase their memories."

"*What?*" Tenley grabbed her head. "You can't erase my memory. I need to know who I am at the ANMIT auditions. What if I think I'm someone else? Like someone who can juggle or something. I can't juggle."

Gavron reached into his tool belt. "I'll do it."

"Gavron," Laraby said. "Put those away. We can't let her see those."

"Who?" Tenley asked. "You mean that old lady in the ugly jumpsuit? *She's* the evil queen?"

"Mother Nature," Gavron said. "She's trying to kill you."

"*That* was Mother Nature? You didn't tell me she wore a *jumpsuit*?" Tenley turned to Pennie.

"Okay. Every single one of you is sounding bonkers." Holden backed away.

Pennie leaned into Laraby. "If we're going to erase their

memory *anyway*? What's the harm in telling them?"

Laraby considered. "All right. But keep it PG. Nothing too gory."

Pennie turned back to Holden. "That old lady *is* Mother Nature. And Gavron's right, she's not very pleased with what's happening to her planet. That's where we come in. We protect you from her, as best we can."

"That's the stupidest thing I've ever heard," Holden snorted.

"I know, right?" Tenley rolled her eyes.

"Ha!" Gavron clapped, thoroughly entertained now. "And you think *my* boys are dumb."

Laraby crossed his arms over his belly and lifted his brow. "What exactly is *stupid* about what Fair One Pennie has just told you?"

Holden grinned. "First of all, Mother Nature isn't real. That's just a made-up term for, you know, like weather and plants and stuff. And second of all, that's just like, stupid."

Laraby studied him. "So, the sudden influx of storms and floods and hurricanes and tornadoes and sinkholes, these are all *random* occurrences?"

Holden shrugged. "Yeah. It's called global warming."

"More like a global meltdown." Gavron slurped.

Pennie stepped closer to Holden. "It's the truth."

Holden snickered. "Then that would mean you were just pretending to be a teenager."

Pennie blinked at him.

"You were *pretending* to be a teenager?"

"I'm sorry, Holden."

"Were you pretending not to know how to skateboard?"

"No." Pennie shook her head. "I can't skateboard."

A loud explosion went off in the distance. Gavron dropped to the ground and covered his ears.

"Time to get out of here," Laraby said.

"Didn't I already say that?" Tenley muttered.

"Time," Laraby said to himself, turning the crystal eight over in his palm. "How does one find time?"

"What are you saying?" Pennie asked him.

"Time," he repeated, louder. "We need to figure out where it is."

"Duh. Time is, like, in the air," Tenley shrugged.

Laraby stared at her. "Time *is*, like, in the air."

Tenley nodded. "Yeah. That's, like, what I just said."

"What are you thinking, Lar?" Pennie asked.

"That I'm a poet and don't even know it?" Tenley beamed.

"Does anyone hear that?" Holden asked, nervously. "That buzzing?"

Tenley collapsed. "I can't go through that again."

There it was, that same buzzing.

"Laraby," Pennie elbowed him. "What is going on?"

"We need to turn back time."

"We *can't*."

"We *can*. We're not on Earth and we're not in Fair City. The Manual says nothing about turning back time in Mother Nature's garden."

Pennie grinned. "That's true."

"Here." He handed her the crystal eight. "Time is in the air.

Slip it in anywhere."

"Anywhere?"

"*Anywhere*," he whispered, flicking his eyes to the right. And in full voice he said, "Say, *Pennie*. Why don't you look for an exit *that way?*" He pointed to the right. Pennie ducked around some trees. "And Gavron?" He walked over to him, still on the ground covering his ears.

"Is the explosion over?" Gavron looked up.

"Yes. Why don't you go look for an exit that way." He pointed to the left. "We need to spread out."

Gavron hurried away, but then thought better of it. "Wait a minute. What about that necklace?"

Just then, a huge gust of wind blew Tenley off the ground. She landed hard on a pile of leaves. Holden pulled her up with his good arm.

"Found the exit!" Pennie yelled. "Over here."

They hurried toward Pennie's voice and stopped short in front of elevator doors rippling in the air, hovering a foot off the ground. The crystal eight was sticking into the middle of it.

"Whoa, a hologram elevator?" Holden smiled.

Tenley crossed her arms. "I'm not going on any more rides. I'll take the stairs." She looked around doubtfully.

"This is the only way out." Laraby walked up to the doors and slipped his hand inside of it. It looked like he had stuck it under rushing water.

Another gust of wind slammed into them. Everyone stayed on their feet this time, but the buzzing grew louder.

Tenley started whimpering. "Please. Make it go away."

"Your stopwatch, Pennie," Laraby said. "Exactly what time did it stop when the Fair Force arrived?"

"Seven fifty-nine and fifty-three seconds."

"That's the time we'll have to go back to. Can I have it?"

Pennie slipped off the stopwatch and handed it to him.

"Okay, you two first." Laraby waved Holden and Tenley up to the doors.

"Watch out!" Holden yelled. But it was too late. Gavron snatched the crystal and sprinted away.

The doors disintegrated.

39

Mother Nature's Garden

Gavron ran for the tall grass.

"See you later, bro!"

A couple of steps and one hidden tree stump later, Gavron flew through the air and landed on his belly. The crystal eight landed to the right of him. Before he could get it again, Holden made a dive for it.

"This is *Pennie's*." Holden grabbed it and stood gripping his cast.

Gavron crawled away. Holden rushed back to Laraby and handed him the crystal.

Laraby stuck it into the air again and another set of doors appeared.

"That is *awesome*," Holden said. "Seriously cool."

"Okay, you two, let's try it again." Laraby waved Tenley up to the new set of doors. Just before she reached it, a black cloud appeared behind her. It hovered above her for a second before diving toward her feet and flipping her onto her back.

Another black cloud appeared behind Holden and did the same. He landed with a violent bounce next to Tenley.

Laraby dropped down to help them. Gavron saw his next opportunity. He sprinted over and plucked out the crystal eight again.

"Boys!" he ordered. The three sipLips hiding behind a tree popped out. "Catch!"

Before Gavron could throw the key, the sipLips blew backwards, splattering against the tree trunk.

"Boys!" Gavron started for them. He hadn't taken a full step when another black cloud appeared, this time above him. It hovered for a moment, then circled around his robes fast enough to lift him off the ground and flip him sideways. He dropped the key.

Laraby scooped it up again. Two trees over, wind was pounding down on Pennie while she clung to a branch.

Holden, who had managed to get to his feet again, extended his good arm to Tenley. She took it and the two pushed onward against the heavy wind together, back to Laraby.

"As soon as the clients are inside the travel box, you're next, Fair One. I'll follow," Laraby shouted to Pennie.

"No!" Pennie yelled back. "Get the sipLips in next. If they don't get to the Log Ride at the same time, they'll be no one to catch Tenley and Holden when they fall over it again."

Holden and Tenley were almost to the doors when Tenley

was blown off her feet, this time six feet in the air. She crumpled to the ground.

"Tenley!" Pennie stormed her way over to her. When she reached her, she pulled her behind the nearest tree. "Are you okay?" She propped Tenley up against the trunk. Tenley's lips were trembling. She looked at Pennie with tears in eyes and shook her head. "My ankle. I can't walk."

"All right, listen to me, Tenley. I'm going to get you out of here. I promise."

"Is this really happening?" Tenley whimpered. "Everything you said about Mother Nature trying to get rid of us?"

"Yes. It is. It's really happening."

Pennie peeked around the trunk. Holden and Laraby were hugging two tree trunks, struggling to hang on. The rippling doors to the travel box were getting dimmer. "What's going on with the doors?" she yelled.

"They're starting to shrink," Laraby shouted. "And it's taking the crystal with it."

Pennie tucked back behind the tree. "We're going to have to make a run for it, Tenley."

"I can't," she said. "Just leave me. I've been such a jerk to you, anyway. I did that remix, Pennie. It was me. I wanted to trend. So I could get more votes. I'm so sorry."

Pennie was struck. But there was no time to think about it now. "Tenley, I'd never leave you. It's my job to protect you."

A tear rolled down Tenley's cheek.

Pennie pulled her up and wrapped her arm around her shoulder. "Now look. Imagine you're late for the ANMIT auditions. They're just about to call your name and you're still in the parking lot. We're going to have to sprint as fast as we can if you're going to make it up to the stage in time. Got it?"

A fierce look came over Tenley. "Got it. I haven't been wearing this ugly sash for nothing."

"Let's go!"

They leapt out from the tree. The wind hit them square on but they held tightly to one other, clenching their teeth and plowing their way to the travel box. A black cloud appeared overhead. Even with the wind whipping past them, they could hear the buzzing.

Holden tugged on a branch, which ripped off easily. He hurled it at the cloud. "Not this time!"

The black cloud broke apart into thousands of bees. Pennie yelped when the first bee stung her. She pulled Tenley into a bear hug to protect her.

"Tenley's allergic to bees!" She yelled to Holden. "Can you get them away from us?"

Another one stung Pennie.

Tenley was shaking uncontrollably now.

"Hold on!" Holden ripped off more branches and opened fire on the bees. Finally, after too many direct hits, the bees zoomed away in different directions, a few of them slamming into each other and dropping to the ground.

"It's clear, go!" Holden called out.

"Hurry!" Laraby waved to them.

"Come on, Tenley," Pennie said.

"But you got stung," she cried. Already, welts were growing on Pennie's cheek and arm.

"Rude little things, aren't they?" Pennie clutched Tenley tighter while they fought their way through the wind.

When they reached the doors, the pink petal was just landing in the trees above them and a new swarm of bees had surrounded it.

"That's her," Holden said. "The lady in the jumpsuit."

Laraby took Tenley's other arm and helped her hobble up next to Holden.

"Both of you!" he ordered. "Get into the box!"

Another thick black cloud blew over Pennie. It hovered for a moment before diving toward her legs and flipping her off her feet. Pennie sailed through the air before smashing into a tree trunk and collapsing onto the ground.

"Pennie!" Tenley shrieked. "Are you okay?"

Pennie's head was spinning and her elbow felt like it was on fire. She waved anyway. "I'm fine."

"She's not okay," Holden told Laraby. "We have to help her."

"You two need to get inside those doors *now*," Laraby demanded. "I will help her once you're safe."

"I can't leave Pennie," Tenley pleaded.

"Listed to me very carefully," Laraby said. "We're sending you back to the Log Ride. To the exact moment when you, Holden, reached out for Tenley before falling over the waterfall."

"That's not possible," Holden said.

"Promise me that you'll grab onto Tenley's ankle. You *have* to be holding onto her when you fall. Promise me?"

"Yeah. Of course. But why do we have to do that again? We could have died."

"You're just going to have to trust me on this, Holden."

"What about Pennie?" Tenley cried. "My mom would kill me if I left her, Pennie! Please, can we wait?"

"Listen to Laraby," Pennie shouted up to her. "You have to believe us. If she gets either one of you in the web again, she won't let you go this time."

"Pennie's right," Laraby said. "Time for you to go. Holden, remember, we're counting on you."

Holden nodded solemnly, took Tenley's arm, and helped her through the fading doors.

"One more thing, Holden!"

Holden turned back.

Laraby pulled the crystal eight out of the air and pressed it inside Holden's palm just before the doors closed.

Laraby's arm was caught. He hit the door with his free hand but the travel box started pulling him off the ground.

"Laraby!" Pennie shrieked, running to him. She wrapped her arms around his waist and yanked. Her legs began lifting off the ground too.

"Let go, Fair One!" Laraby begged her. "Save yourself!"

"No!" Pennie yelled.

They were a few meters off the ground now. Pennie wouldn't be able to hold on much longer. And even if she could, the travel box was disintegrating rapidly. Laraby's arm, and perhaps the rest of him, would disintegrate along with it.

Two filthy sleeves wrapped around Pennie's waist.

"I got you, Fairly One."

"Gavron!"

"This might hurt a little, bro." Keeping one arm around Pennie, Gavron reached up and grabbed onto Laraby. He yanked hard enough for Laraby to cry out in pain. His arm still wouldn't budge.

"Boys!" Gavron screamed. Before Pennie realized what was happening, she was propelling through the air with the three sipLips. They dropped her on the ground and returned to Gavron. Pennie watched the sipLips encircle Gavron, who had both arms wrapped around Laraby's waist. The sipLips began circling fast enough to create a small wind tunnel.

After a small blast, the travel box was gone.

Out of the vapor, five spinning bodies fell. The sipLips landed on top of each other and scurried away. Gavron and Laraby landed a few meters away.

"Holy Helium," Gavron groaned, pushing Laraby off him. "Would it kill you to lay off on the froyo, bro, yo?"

Laraby rubbed his arm and tried to collect himself. "I hadn't anticipated that. Thank you, Gavron."

"No worries," Gavron said, winking at Pennie. "It's what we heroes do."

An eerie silence descended upon the garden. The buzzing, the wind—all the noise, had come to a complete stop.

Gavron pointed up. "Um. I think you need to see this, bro."

Pennie saw it before Laraby did. The bees above them had shaped themselves into an arrow, aimed directly for them.

Under his breath, as quietly as he could, Laraby said, "Pennie, come closer. Gavron. Get your boys over here right now."

Pennie crawled closer and Gavron waved to the sipLips who

were peeking out from around a tree. They zoomed over.

"Stay together, everyone. Gavron, keep a tight hold on Pennie."

"Your command is my wish come true," he gurgled, wrapping Pennie into his grimy robes with him.

Laraby pulled the *Tornado* bottle out of his pocket.

"You're not really going to use that," Pennie said.

Laraby shook the bottle.

"Those things got some serious momentum, bro. Not sure we can survive it."

"Only one way to find out." Laraby popped the cork.

A tornado tore out of the bottle. Pennie, Laraby, Gavron, and the three screaming sipLips shot upward inside it.

40

00:00:07
Adventures, Inc. Again

Six figures spit out of the tornado and onto the ground just in time to see Holden lunge for Tenley's ankle at the top of the waterfall.

"Get 'em, boys!" Gavron threw the dizzy sipLips toward the Log Ride.

But the tornado got there first.

The tornado ripped through the Log Ride, sucking in first Tenley and then Holden.

The sipLips flew off empty-handed, shaking their heads and shrugging their shoulders.

"No!" Pennie yelled. After everything she'd done, she still couldn't save Tenley. She and Holden were both going to end up dead.

A lightning bolt shot out of the tornado and across the sky.

On top of it, two figures were wrapped together.

"Is that—"

The lightning bolt headed straight for the roller coaster.

"How could—" Laraby stuttered.

The two figures launched themselves off the lightning bolt and landed directly inside one of the roller coaster cars, still chugging its way up the backside of the rails, out of the tornado's path.

Before the roller coaster disappeared over the other side, the two figures clambered upright and sank into their seats.

Pennie turned to Laraby. "I think Holden—"

"Just discovered his element," Laraby finished.

"Well, that's dandy news for the gravity-gropers, but less dandy for us." Gavron pointed to the tornado, which had changed course and was heading straight for them now.

Pennie backed up. "Uh, Lar?"

Laraby threw his arms up. "I've got nothing."

Gavron activated his propellers. For a moment, it looked like he was going to abandon the Fair Ones. "I want every last copy of that video, bro. And your promise to never bring it up again. Is that a deal?"

"Deal!" Laraby agreed.

"A hero's work is never done," Gavron said, pulling them both into his spinning vortex. "Let's go, boys!"

The mass of swirling Fair Ones and sipLips lifted away split seconds before the tornado reached them.

41

Fair City

"Watch where you're going." A Fair One glared at Pennie. *Abe's Tool Shine* was on the back of his robes.

"Sorry." Pennie stepped around him and resumed her pace up the grand staircase. After acclimating to gravity, she could run circles around the other Fair Ones.

"I'm not even panting!" Pennie called up to Laraby who stood waiting under the entrance of City Hall.

"Let me do the talking," he said.

Pennie followed Laraby to the Tool Belt Check. The same teen Administrator with the eyebrow piercing chewed loudly her gum.

"Hello. My friend here needs to pick up her tool belt."

"Ticket?" She held out her hand.

"She lost it."

"Can't help you then," the teen said.

"However." Laraby rocked back and forth on his toes. "I have remotely programmed the Intel inside one of the Fair One's devices. So if you'll stand aside, a locker will open on its own."

The teen frowned at him. A locker in the top row popped open.

The teen handed Pennie her tool belt, chanking extra loudly on her gum. "That's pretty cool," she said. "Never seen no one do that before."

"Why, thank you." Laraby bowed.

The alarm sounded.

"No propellers!" Gavron groaned, shaking his head at the three small sipLips, unrecognizable in their crisp white robes and shiny clean faces, huddled in the doorway. "De-activate, boys!" They did. Laraby turned to the teen. "I'm very sorry about that. They are a little rambunctious. It won't happen again. Will it, boys?"

The sipLips giggled and drooled.

Laraby leaned down to them. "Okay, outside. And remember, stay on the stairs. *No leaving the stairs*. Or there's no mini moon golf. Do you hear me?"

The sipLips saluted and slurped before spinning out the door.

Pennie buckled her tool belt, which felt a little snugger after all of Mrs. Tylwyth's cooking. "Three days, Lar? I would have thought Gavron would make you watch them for at least a week in exchange of your tools back."

Laraby shifted his tool belt and grumbled. "He kept the froyo maker."

251

"Maybe that was a good idea." Pennie nodded at his belly.

The Great Hall was packed, once again. Grumpy, sweating Fair Ones were squeezed shoulder to shoulder.

"What's going on in here?" Pennie asked.

"Big announcement," a scruffy Fair One answered. "Original Eights called us all in."

Laraby looked down at his tablet. "It's true. I just got the notice."

Pennie pulled out her own device. *ALL FAIR ONES REPORT TO CITY HALL IMMEDIATELY*, flashed on the screen.

"Must be big." Laraby nodded up to a stage floating under the hologram clock. *May His Return be Swift* was still lit brightly over the hours, minutes and seconds since the Super had been gone.

"If there's eight of em, why are there only seven chairs?" the scruffy Fair One tsked.

"Because technically—" Laraby started.

"No time, Lar." Pennie pulled him away and dragged him through the crowd to the back exit, where she led him down the hallway.

"Room Seventy-one is this way."

No one answered. Pennie knocked on the door again. "Tink? Maybe she's in Command Center."

Pennie steered Laraby around the corner and down another hall.

"Look for a break in the wall," Pennie told him.

"Like this one?" Laraby pointed.

"That's it."

Inside, rows of Fairs Force were seated on wind seats

monitoring the enormous hologram screens.

Laraby froze. "This. Is. Amazing."

Pennie yanked him in farther. "Tink and I sat back there."

A familiar figure walked toward them.

"Lord Fairship." Pennie stopped.

"Yes, hello," Lord Fairship smiled. "And how may I be of service?"

"Your Fairship. My name's Fair One PENN 1. I met you before my travels to Earth for a Right to Delete?"

"Oh yes." Lord Fairship clasped his hands together.

"PENN 1, is that you?" Tink slipped around from behind him. "All went well, we heard?"

Pennie noticed Lady Fairship a few steps back, her eyes narrowed tightly.

"We're just going out for an announcement," Tink said. "You'll need to be there as well, I believe."

"This won't take long, Tink. I promise. My friend and I—you know Fair One LARA B3."

Laraby dipped his head. "Your Fairships."

Lady Fairship glared at her. Pennie swallowed. "We came to tell you about something that happened during the trip."

Lady Fairship's pupils flattened into straight lines. Pennie opened her mouth to say more, but nothing came out.

Laraby saw the look of terror on Pennie's face and took over. "Right. Something that we don't think you know about. Something only Lady Fairship knows about, in fact."

Lord Fairship smiled. "I think Lady Fairship's told us everything. A few times over."

"And a few more times after that," Tink agreed. "A successful Right to Delete we are told!"

Lady Fairship shifted her snake eyes to Laraby.

He cleared his throat. "Did Lady Fairship tell you that she tried to get Fair One PENN 1 to delete her *identity*?"

Lady Fairship's face hardened. One of her snake eyes twitched.

Lord Fairship shuffled forward. "Whatever are you talking about, Fair One? We don't allow that. You may want to check it in the Manual."

"Rule number three, section 5228: *Never shall a Fair One be ordered to delete his or her identity,*" Laraby recited. "*Anyone who tries to do so will be banished.*"

Lord Fairship looked impressed with him. "Indeed."

Lady Fairship only glared harder.

"Is this true, Lady Fairship?" Tinktoria asked.

"Yes." Lady Fairship cleared her throat. "I'm afraid it is."

Pennie and Laraby exchanged a quick look. Lord Fairship raised his brow.

"Of course," Lady Fairship continued, with her eyes trained on Pennie. "This is the necessary order of events when a Fair One is promoted to Lieutenant Fair One."

Laraby's jaw dropped. He looked at Pennie.

"A rookie Fair One promoted to a *Lieutenant* Fair One?" Tinktoria asked. "That's unheard of."

"Until now," Lady Fairship said. "You see, what I saw her accomplish on Earth, the way she got her client to agree to the Right to Delete without so much as an argument, well," she

254

paused, "Fair One PENN 1 is one of the most capable Fair Ones in Fair City." Lady Fairship attempted a smile.

"Oh well! Very good then." Lord Fairship clapped. "Congratulations, Fair One PENN 1." He shook Pennie's hand.

Lady Fairship stepped closer to Pennie. "It is wonderful. But I am still awaiting her response. She has yet to officially accept the honor." She frowned tightly at Pennie. "So tell us, PENN 1, have you decided to accept the promotion?"

Pennie opened her mouth and closed it again. She looked at Tink and then Laraby. And finally back to Lady Fairship. "My answer depends on whether or not there are *two* promotions available. You see, LARA B3 is just as deserving as I am. More, in fact."

Lady Fairship's face grew dark. Over her shoulder, Lord Fairship's face brightened. "Well, that sounds reasonable. I have to say I do agree. Lady Fairship?"

Lady Fairship stared deep into Pennie's eyes. "Yes, he most certainly is. Both of you shall be promoted to Lieutenant Fair One."

A noise fell out of Laraby. Girl-like. "A 3rdi-All," he squeaked. "A 3rdi-All."

"Excellent!" Lord Fairship said, shaking Laraby's hand this time.

"There is one more thing," Pennie continued, without breaking eye contact with Lady Fairship. "I haven't yet been reassigned to a new client, now that my old client's Right to Delete is complete, and she no longer needs my protection, and all."

A flicker of worry spread across Lady Fairship's brow.

"Luckily," Pennie smiled. "I do happen to know of a client in need of protection. I believe you know of her too, Lady Fairship? She saved a little girl from drowning? Her previous Fair One was told to stay—"

"Yes! I know you who mean. Thank you for reminding me." She glanced at Dan Ringer standing a few feet behind. "Commander? Can you take care of this right away? Assigning this client to PENN 1?"

He entered something into his tablet. "It has been arranged, Your Fairship."

Pennie's tool belt pinged. She pulled her tablet out. A picture of Tenley Tylwyth's face with *New Client* and her critical information below stared back at her.

"Perfect," Tenley said, slipping the tablet back in her belt. "This is exactly who I was thinking of. Thank you, Lady Fairship."

"Now if you'll excuse us," Lady Fairship pushed forward, taking Lord Fairship's arm. "We have a very important announcement to get to, and we can't keep the Fair Ones waiting any longer."

Laraby and Pennie moved to the side to let the Fairships pass. When Tinktoria reached her, Pennie stepped forward. "Tink, there's something else I need to tell you."

"I'm afraid it will have to wait, Fair One. I mean future *Lieutenant* Fair One." Tink gave her a hasty smile and hurried out the door after the other Fairships.

Laraby shook his head. "It worked. You managed to threaten exposing Lady Fairship's attempt to remove your identity in exchange for getting Tenley back as your client. *And* you got us both promoted to Lieutenant Fair One. Lady Fairship is right, you *are* the most capable Fair One in Fair City."

"And you'll make the most capable *Lieutenant* Fair One in Fair City," Pennie said.

Laraby's face fell.

"What is it?"

"Your persuasive talents aside, she did cave awfully fast. Do you think Lady Fairship might be hiding something bigger than just trying to get your identity erased?"

"Like what kind of bigger?"

"I'm not sure." Laraby gave one last glance around Command Center. "We better get out there for the announcement," he said. "Hopefully Gavron hasn't done something worth announcing."

Before they stepped into the Great Hall, Laraby stopped. "What you did for me, Fair One Pennie, I can't begin to express my gratitude for. Thank you."

Pennie smirked. "Don't thank me yet. You might be making the biggest mistake of your life."

42

Hadley Beach

Principal Frimpy clapped too hard into the microphone and smiled down at his notes, unaware that most of the students and parents were covering their ears. Behind him, at the back of the stage, a long *Congratulations, Graduates!* sign hung between two bouquets of balloons.

"Congratulations again, eighth-grade graduates," Principal Frimpy said, placing his hands on either side of the podium. "Now before we let you go, we do have one final order of business. Most of you know that Mr. Mingby and his students were caught in a horrible tornado. Our thoughts are with all the affected families.

One of our own Hadley Middle School students performed a magnificent act of courage that saved a young girl from drowning. This student's actions were, and why should I be surprised, captured on video and immediately put on social medial. *This time* however, producing a *positive* result for our community. So let's bring her up as our Hometown Hero. Tenley Tylwyth. You know her as our official nominee for *America's Next Most Inspirational Teen!*"

The crowd erupted into a standing ovation.

Tenley straightened her new official *ANMIT Nominee* sash as she started down the aisle, limping slightly. Behind her, sitting on her father's shoulders, little Emmie smiled and kicked Mrs. Tylwyth accidentally, who stood next to them holding the toddler. They all cheered for Tenley.

At the podium, Mr. Frimpy shook Tenley's hand and gave her the microphone.

"Thank you so much everyone for voting for me, Tenley T, as Hadley Beach's official nominee for *America's Next Most Inspirational Teen!*"

Cheers erupted again. In the crowd, Ms. Shareen whistled through her fingers. Mr. Mingby wrapped his arm around her proudly.

"And I hope everyone watched my nail art tutorial on tiny tornadoes." She held up her hand to show ten different tornadoes on each of her nails. "While I'm super excited and grateful to be Hadley Beach's official nominee," her voice cracked. "I can't accept it."

Hushed tones fell across the crowd.

"The thing is, there's someone out there who deserves it more than me. Someone who I never even *noticed* before. Because let's face it, he's someone who isn't very tall or even that hot yet." Tenley smiled. "But this person had to think really quickly and concentrate really hard to save us during that tornado, putting himself in danger when he could have just let me fall." Tenley pulled off her sash. "So, while I still hope you'll all watch my nail art tutorial next week," she lowered her voice, "think three-dimensional letters," then again in full voice, "I hereby give you Hadley Beach's *new* official nominee for *America's Next Most Inspiration Teen*, Holden Wonderbolt!"

Holden looked like a deer caught in headlights. A row down from Mrs. Tylwyth, he shook his head and waved the applause away, but the crowed started chanting his name, louder and louder, until finally he had no choice. He stood and walked down the aisle and onto the stage.

"Tenley, what are you doing?" he whispered.

Tenley dropped the sash over his shoulder and cinched it around his waist. The crowd chanted, "Speech! Speech! Speech!"

Tenley pushed him forward to the podium.

"Um, so, yeah." He nodded to the crowd. "I was, you know, just glad to be able to help out. And hopefully there won't be too many more tornados in Southern California."

He waved and stepped off the podium. The students chanted, "Wonder-bolt! Wonder-bolt!"

Principal Frimpy took back the podium. "And that concludes our ceremony. Happy summer, everybody. Remember, do something good and see something great!"

Mrs. Tylwyth rushed up to the stage with the squirming toddler. "That was sweet, Tenley," she smiled. "Holden dear, have you heard anything from Pennie?"

"No," Holden answered. "I haven't."

Mrs. Tylwyth blinked back tears. "I wish she'd come home." She turned back up the aisle.

Holden and Tenley stepped off the stage together.

"Ow." Tenley hopped on her good foot.

"I keep forgetting about your ankle," Holden said.

Tenley looked down at his cast. "Guess that makes us even."

"Guess so," he agreed, starting up the aisle.

When they reached the auditorium exit, they stood at the doorway and looked up at the sky.

"Hey Holden, do you think Pennie's ever coming back?"

"I don't know. Everyone made so much fun of her."

"I'd never let anyone make fun of her again."

"Me neither," Holden said. In the distance, a quick flash of lightning lit up the sky.

He slipped his hand into his pocket and curled his fingers around the crystal eight.

ACKNOWLEDGEMENTS

I grew up in a house full of art and creativity and for that I am forever thankful to my mother, Jinxie. My father, John Gooch, besides being the best dad on the face of the planet, also taught me how to act nice, eat rice, and let the good times roll—which comes in handier than you might think. Building a story world takes many eyes on the page and I am grateful for my editor, Tara Creel, my bff, Jessica Benjamin, my publisher, Georgia McBride, and my agent, Jennifer Unter. My mostly-delightful daughters, Madison, Daisy and Tatum (who gave me the bottle idea) are proof that I'm the luckiest mom in the world; and my husband, Craig, never gives up on us—even when we go all Tenley Tylwyth on him.

JENNIFER GOOCH HUMMER

Jennifer Gooch Hummer is the award-winning author and screenwriter for her debut novel, GIRL UNMOORED. Raised in Boston, Jennifer graduated from Kenyon College with a B.A. in English and moved to Los Angeles where she read scripts for major talent agencies and production companies. A true believer in fairies, Jennifer currently lives in Southern California with her whistling husband, three teenage daughters, and two slightly neurotic rescue dogs.

OPERATION TENLEY is the first book in the series, THE FAIR CITY FILES.

Connect with Jennifer - http://jennifergoochhummer.com

OTHER MONTH9BOOKS TITLES YOU MIGHT LIKE

HAIR IN ALL THE WRONG PLACES
UN/FAIR
POPPY MAYBERRY, THE MONDAY

Find more books like this at Month9Books.com

Connect with Month9Books online:

Facebook: www.Facebook.com/Month9Books
Twitter: https://twitter.com/Month9Books
You Tube: www.youtube.com/user/Month9Books
Tumblr: http://month9books.tumblr.com/
Instagram: https://instagram.com/month9books

ANDREW BUCKLEY
HAIR IN ALL THE WRONG PLACES
WHAT'S HAPPENING TO HIM? WHAT HAS HE DONE?
AND WHAT ON EARTH IS THAT SMELL?

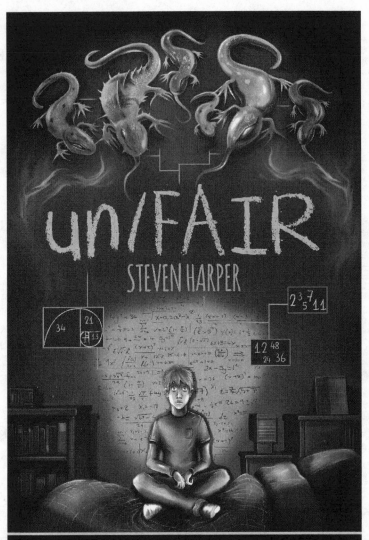

un/FAIR

STEVEN HARPER

BETWEEN REALITY AND FANTASY
LIES THE RATHER FRIGHTENING TRUTH

Monday isn't just another day of the week.

Poppy Mayberry, The Monday

NOVA KIDS BOOK 1

Jennie K. Brown